EGMONT

A TRAGEDY IN FIVE ACTS

GOETHE

EGMONT

A Tragedy in Five Acts

TRANSLATED FROM THE GERMAN BY WILLARD R. TRASK

INTRODUCTION BY ALEXANDER GODE VON AESCH

NEW ENGLAND INSTITUTE
OF TECHNOLOGY
LEARNING RESOURCES CENTER

BARRON'S EDUCATIONAL SERIES, INC.

WOODBURY, NEW YORK

INTRODUCTION

On October 1, 1788, Goethe noted in a letter to his friend and patron, the Grand-Duke Charles Augustus of Saxe Weimar: "There is a review of my *Egmont* in the Literary Gazette, which analyzes quite nicely the moral part of the play. As for the poetic part, I suspect the reviewer has left a few things for someone else to add."

This reviewer, not further identified in Goethe's letter, was Schiller. The review itself had appeared in the *Jenaer Allgemeine Literaturzeitung* of September 20, 1788.

It was more than five years later that a chance meeting of Schiller and Goethe laid the foundation of their friendship which later generations have come to regard as an innate necessity of history. When Schiller wrote his review of Goethe's *Egmont,* a different kind of chance occurrence might well have driven the two great men into mutually hostile positions.

Schiller judged *Egmont* as a character tragedy and found it wanting. This was inevitable. His dramatic sense permitted him to recognize only three varieties of tragic conflict: one determined by extraordinary actions or situations, another determined by human passion, and a third determined by character.

The situation in *Egmont* is that of the historical conflicts leading up to the rebellion of the Netherlands against

Spain. Schiller was quick to acknowledge the superb mas
tery with which Goethe had handled every detail of local
color. The opening scene, in which the citizens of Brussels,
gathered on the occasion of an outdoor shooting contest,
epitomize the play as a whole—including time and place,
the hero's character, and his tragic end—struck Schiller as
worthy of Shakespeare and reminded him forcibly of the
mass scenes in *Julius Caesar*. But it was obvious to Schiller
—and should be to anyone else—that *Egmont* was not written because Goethe wanted to glorify the heroic struggle
of the Netherlanders for their freedom. If that had been his
purpose, he would have allowed more action (of which
there was plenty around at that particular time) to appear
on the stage instead of pushing it into the background and
alluding to it only as having already occurred.

It was still more obvious to Schiller—and remains so to
any modern reader—that *Egmont* cannot be construed as
a tragedy of passion. There just is no passion in it. There
is Clara's love for Egmont and Egmont's love for Clara.
But while it is certainly true that the delicate tenderness of
the love scenes in *Egmont* is hard or impossible to match
in its direct and truly naive simplicity, there is no passionate conflict here. This love would be idyllic if it were not
for the fact that Egmont falls victim to the wiles of his enemy, Alba, and that Clara is unable to live on when there
is no hope left for the life of her lover.

So Schiller had to conclude that the tragedy in *Egmont*
lies in the character of the hero. But starting from this

premise he was bound to arrive at some shocking conclusions.

For three years Schiller had been working on his *History of the Secession of the Netherlands* of which Part I (the only part ever published) went to press at about the time when he wrote his review of Goethe's *Egmont*. Thus Schiller was quite familiar with the subject matter and saw immediately what striking liberties Goethe had permitted himself in his portrayal of the Count of Egmont and Prince of Gavre. In historical reality, this man, born in 1522, was 45 years old at the time of his execution in 1567. He was solidly married and had eight or eleven children. Both he and his wife had expensive tastes, and it seems that the major reason for his refusal to run for his life away from Brussels (as Orange so wisely and successfully did, followed by several others whom Alba would have liked to execute together with Egmont) was simply that he depended for the support of his large family on his local sources of income. Exile, voluntary or otherwise, would have meant poverty, and poverty was a luxury he could ill afford.

Now, Schiller did not object to the fact that Goethe had changed all this. What he found shocking was the direction in which the changes had been made. It seemed excusable that the staid middle-aged family man had been turned into an ebullient bachelor in early manhood. It was even all right for this youthful hero to be given a bourgeois mistress contrary to historical truth. What was not all right, in Schiller's view, was the fact that all these deviations from history did not heighten in any way the tragic appeal of Egmont's character.

A family man risking his life in order to provide decently for wife and children is surely not the most sublime of all possible tragic characters, but compared to Goethe's Egmont he might seem so. Goethe's Egmont is charmingly in love. This love makes him "blind," puts him in a mood of "foolish confidence"—these are Schiller's words—and when we expect him to do something heroic to take a stand against the dark powers that threaten his life, he is not on hand, he hasn't the time, for he has promised his girl to spend the evening with her.

Instead of heightening the tragic potential in Egmont's character, the changes Goethe effected in his historic model have reduced that potential to practically zero. This, in essence, was Schiller's complaint. It seems to have remained the leitmotiv down through the ensuing decades of most critical attacks on Goethe's *Egmont*.

To all of which Goethe replied that the criticism might seem sound in moral terms but that there remained a few things to be added in poetic terms. What are they?

II

Egmont is one of the three major works in dramatic form conceived by Goethe during the early years of his Storm and Stress, the period before he left Frankfurt in November 1775, at the age of 26, for a short visit to Weimar, which subsequently was extended to almost 57 years, till his death in 1832.

All three of these works, *Götz von Berlichingen, Faust,* and *Egmont,* were conceived in emulation of Shakespeare —whether rightly or wrongly understood does not matter— as quick successions of lively scenes, without concern for the requirements of the contemporary stage and in open rebellion against Aristotelian or French or Gallicized German dramatic theory.

Götz was completed and published in this spirit (1773). Its amazing vitality on the stage is not the result of a playwright's superior skill. Goethe himself called the work a "dramatized story." It lives so powerfully because we can't help sensing how much Goethe liked that old roughneck Götz, and so we like him too.

Faust became Goethe's life work. In its final form this Divine Comedy of modern man stands as a towering mountain. As the historian of literature faces it like a probing geologist, intent upon establishing order and sequence in this welter of strata, he finds but one—the oldest—to be igneous rock of Götz-like origin.

Egmont falls between the two extremes of *Götz* and *Faust.* It is, like *Götz,* a loose-jointed sequence of scenes rather than a well-constructed drama, but the young genius responsible for it was obviously no longer convinced that every kind of discipline was necessarily of the devil. If the whole of *Götz* had stepped, as it were, out of an old book which Goethe happened to come across and devoured in youthful enthusiasm, *Egmont,* on the other hand, reflects a good deal of historical search, of composition, of poetic invention, and—in a word—of hard work.

Goethe's major sources for his *Egmont* were a history of the rebellion of the Netherlands by the Dutchman, Emanuel van Meteren, which he read in a seventeenth-century German translation, and a work by the Jesuit, Famianus Strada, which he read in the Latin original. We have seen with what unconcern Goethe treated his sources, and we may well assert that he used them to lend substance to a vision he had—and the vision mattered more than the substance.

After more than ten years in Weimar, in 1786, Goethe went to Italy. It is better to say, he *fled* to Italy where he expected to achieve a rebirth as a creative artist. This desperate desire of his was fulfilled. But if the intervening years of devotion to duty, of scientific search, of technological and bureaucratic organization had not killed the fire of his genius, they had tamed it into subservience to classical ideals of perfection in structure and form. It was in pursuit of such ideals that Goethe went South where so many Germans before him had gone, from Charlemagne to Winckelmann, and when he returned from Italy, he seemed more than a mere dozen years, he seemed ages, away from his exuberant beginnings. He was now the "classical" Goethe, the Goethe of *Iphigenie* (1787) and of *Torquato Tasso* (1790) in which a majestic flow of German

iambs delineates a continuity of logically concise and es-
thetically inspiring action.

And it was in Rome, on September 1, 1787, that Goethe
completed his *Egmont*. That he had worked on it inter-
mittently during the intervening years—in 1778 and 1779
and again in 1781—is not particularly important. The dates
to remember are 1773 (*Götz*) and 1787 (*Iphigenie*), or
better still, remember the differences of dramatic style, in
Götz and *Iphigenie*. In *Egmont,* we find echoes of *Götz* in
the mass scenes and in the happy love scenes of Clara and
Egmont; we find, too, intimations of *Iphigenie,* in the numerous passages of "iambic prose." The latter struck Schiller so forcibly that, in his review of *Egmont,* he had the
printer set one lengthy quotation in the traditional verse
form of iambic pentameters, which were marred by only a
very few metric irregularities.

It is not very surprising that *Egmont* met with little approval when Goethe showed the manuscript to friends upon
his return from Italy and when it appeared in print in 1788.
Charles Augustus just did not like it, but then, his tastes
were essentially French, and if he did admire *Iphigenie,*
one may suspect that he mistook it as being conceived and
executed in the spirit of Racine. Frau von Stein, Goethe's
friend of many years (who never forgave him his "heathen-
ish" life in Rome), called Clara a whore. She was shocked
to find, in the operatic closing scene of the play, the vision
of Freedom in Egmont's dream assuming the features of
that abandoned creature.

The practical reason—artistically unimportant—why Goethe had striven to complete several of his works during his sojourn in Italy was a projected edition of his collected works. *Egmont* appeared in volume V. The whole set was sold on a subscription basis, and there were 602 subscribers to it in all of Germany. In addition, Volume V achieved 487 individual sales, and then there was a separate printing of *Egmont* alone which sold 377 copies. Total sales of *Egmont* in the first edition were thus 1,466 copies. The publisher lost heavily on it, as he did on the whole set.

Egmont was first performed in Weimar on March 31, 1791. The success was indifferent. There was too much *Götz* in the play and not enough *Iphigenie,* or too much *Iphigenie* and not enough *Götz,* depending on the individual spectator's point of view, with the former no doubt predominating at Weimar.

In 1796 Schiller was commissioned by Goethe to prepare a stage version of *Egmont.* He did so, as Goethe put it, "with brutal violence," but the result was a text with stage vitality. It is in Schiller's arrangement that *Egmont* won its place in the repertories of most German theaters and has kept it to this very day. Through Beethoven's music (1810), the name and fame of *Egmont,* though not the play itself, have traveled far abroad.

III

We may well wonder whether Schiller, after 1796, would have written the same kind of review of *Egmont* as he had done eight years before. He learned a great deal through his efforts to arrange the work for the stage. If he had not said so himself in his correspondence with his friend Körner, it would still be apparent to any careful student of his later dramas. The most striking illustrations of this are probably to be found in Schiller's monumental trilogy of *Wallenstein*.

The historical setting of the work, the political intrigues which are its theme, and also the character of its hero are initially presented through their reflection in Wallenstein's camp. This is clearly parallel to the opening scene of *Egmont*, where the citizenry of Brussels performs a similar function of dramatic economy. The son of Wallenstein's principal opponent plays a part quite similar to that of Alba's son Ferdinand, whose admiration and love for Egmont symbolize, in a sense, the latter's ultimate triumph over his executioner. There are numerous such parallels, minor and major, but none seems more significant than the fact that Wallenstein himself is essentially as inactive a hero as Egmont.

It is almost as though Schiller had depicted his Wallenstein as passively ready to accept his fate—whatever the stars had decreed it to be—because he wanted to show that he had understood after all what Goethe had tried to express in his *Egmont*. However, if there is a kernel of truth in this bold supposition, it cannot be supported by so flimsy a base as the fact that Schiller had spent a considerable amount of time and energy on the preparation of a stage arrangement of one of his great friend's dramatic works. The base must rather be found in the friendship itself that linked these two embodiments of opposite poles in thought and emotion.

The chance occurrence which brought Schiller and Goethe together is highly significant for our purposes. For years the two had lived a few miles apart. Finally one day in 1794, they happened to leave together from a lecture given by someone at Jena on some biological subject. To say something to fill the silence between them, Schiller remarked that he did not care too much for so atomistic a treatment of natural phenomena. Goethe replied that he too believed that there were better and sounder ways, and he proceeded to explain to Schiller his conception of the metamorphosis of plants. This led to a lively discussion culminating in Schiller's aggressive remark that this matter of the metamorphosis of plants was neither fact nor experience but an idea. Goethe haughtily replied that he had never known that he had ideas but he was quite pleased to learn better, particularly since it all meant that he had ideas which he could see with his own eyes.

At first sight, this may seem to be a strange foundation for one of the most productive friendships in all human history. But we need to understand that Goethe's doctrine of the metamorphosis of plants was a direct application of his basic, one might say religious, knowledge of the organic structure of all life and all existence. Everything that lives or exists is part of an organism; the part helps to determine the totality of the organism, while in turn, the part is determined by the whole. Call it a principle that stipulates the coincidence of freedom and necessity, of destiny and chance, of endeavor and foregone conclusion—all these are possible illustrations, and none is more cogent or less significant than the others.

This "organic idea," as it has come rather awkwardly to be called, pervades all of Goethe's work as a poet and as a scientist. And, on that day in Jena in 1794, Schiller understood what Goethe was talking about. The fact that Schiller, essentially a thinker, could understand the ideas of Goethe, essentially a seer, was to the latter a confirmation of his theories. To Schiller, the experience meant similarly a justification of his ways.

It should be clear now what Goethe meant when he stated that Schiller's review of his *Egmont* had left to others a few things to be added as far as the poetic part of the work was concerned. To Schiller it was clear after 1794. He expressed it once and for all in his great essay on sentimental and naive poetry. Schiller is sentimental, Goethe naive. The peculiar connotations of the former term need not be explained in this context. As for "naive," remember the etymology of the term. It is cognate with "native" and belongs in the same word family as "nature."

If Schiller had once criticized the *Egmont* poem as lacking in dramatic tension and had explained this lack as a direct result of the "blind" and "foolish" confidence of its hero, we may assume that at a later time he would still have noted the total absence of dramatic tension but that this observation would no longer have been a criticism of the work. He would have seen in it—as we do today—a necessary aspect of the poetic greatness of *Egmont,* which resides in the portrayal of a naive character. For in this sense Egmont is Goethe.

IV

In the final pages of his autobiography, *Of Poetry and Truth* (which he carried to precisely the time of his departure from Frankfurt for Weimar), Goethe projected the wisdom of his mature detachment into the turbulent experiences of those early days of passionate involvement. Then all that happened seemed accident and chance, dependent on subjective whims and irrational events. And yet, in retrospect, it seemed simultaneously determined by an inner necessity full of purpose and awareness of the ultimate outcome.

Ready to leave for Weimar, young Goethe had been bragging to everyone ready, or not so ready, to listen that a duke had invited him to his court and that the duke's carriage was to call for him within a few days. The few days passed, and the duke's carriage failed to arrive. Goethe went into hiding rather than face the humiliation inherent in this absurd situation. But his father, ever distrustful of princely favors, made life miserable for him with his sarcastic I-told-you-so's.

Finally Goethe decided to run away from it all, departing for Italy in the dark of night. He stayed over at Heidelberg for a few days at the home of his good friend, Demoiselle Delf, who had great plans for him and wanted him, after his return from Italy, to make a place for himself in the literary life of the Palatinate. All this was sound and sensible. Goethe's father would have approved of it.

Then suddenly, in the nick of time, a messenger arrived from Frankfurt. The carriage had been delayed and was now on its way. The courtier in charge of it, a certain Herr von Kalb, pleaded with Goethe not to humiliate him before the duke, to accept his apologies, and to join him for the originally projected trip to Weimar. All this was unsound and senseless. Goethe's father would not have approved any more now than he had before.

And yet, Goethe had to reject the advice of reason and the pleadings of Demoiselle Delf. He had to go to Weimar, as though driven by a power that knew what hung in the balance.

In this moment of "foolish confidence" Goethe was acting out his future destiny. The power that guided him at this crucial moment would have been called the gods by the Ancients. The Moderns might call it Providence. Goethe, too, had to give it a name and make of it thus a tangible entity. He called it the daimon.

Now to close the circle, here are the closing lines of Goethe's poem *Sea Voyage*, which was written within the year after his fateful Heidelberg decision.

And with manly strength he holds the rudder.—
Wind and waves are playing with his vessel,
But his heart is not a toy of wind and waves.
Gazing at the yawning depths below him,
He relies, in shipwreck or safe landing,
On his gods.

This seafarer, relying on his gods, trusting (and living and being) his daimon, is Goethe. This seafarer is Goethe and Egmont as well.

In his mature years, both as a scientist and as a poet, Goethe came to be knowingly aware of many facets of the "organic coincidence of chance and necessity." Much of this he owed to Schiller. If *Egmont* remained dear to him to the end, the reason is clearly that he saw in this work (of the years of his coming of age as a creative poet) a remarkably unconscious—in Schiller's terms: a totally naive—delineation of the essence of his being.

On the last pages of his autobiography, Goethe described the pleading comportment of Demoiselle Delf, who tried so hard to make him obey the voice of reason instead of the daimon. He put into his own mouth, as a final and decisive rejoinder, the words which Egmont used to cut off his secretary's plea for caution and reason, which was—as Egmont saw it—a plea against life, against trust, against the daimon: *Child, child! Say no more! As if lashed on by invisible spirits, the Sun-god's coursers of the times carry the light chariot of our destiny on in their headlong gallop; and there is noth-*

ing we can do save, ready and bold, to grasp the reins and guide the wheels now left, now right, here from a rock, there from a plunge. Who knows where he is bound? Scarcely can he remember whence he came.

Did Goethe actually quote his Egmont in this way when talking prose to Demoiselle Delf at Heidelberg? Or did he say something which he subsequently translated into the language of poetry suitable for Egmont? We do not know. And it does not matter.

A.J.G.v.A.

January, 1960

CAST OF CHARACTERS

MARGARET OF PARMA, daughter of Charles V and Regent of the Netherlands.

COUNT EGMONT, Prince of Gavre.

WILLIAM OF ORANGE.

THE DUKE OF ALBA.

FERDINAND, his bastard son.

MACHIAVELLI, secretary to the Regent.

RICHARD, Egmont's secretary.

SILVA, } serving under Alba.
GOMEZ,

CLARA, Egmont's sweetheart.

HER MOTHER.

BRACKENBURG, son of a citizen of Brussels.

SOEST, SHOPKEEPER
JETTER, TAILOR
CARPENTER, } citizens of Brussels.
SOAPMAKER,

BUYCK, soldier under Egmont.

RUYSUM, old soldier, disabled and deaf.

VANSEN, a scribe.

People, attendants, guards, etc.

The scene is in Brussels.

ACT I

❲❳

SCENE ONE

Crossbowmen's Contest. Soldiers and Citizens (with cross-bows), JETTER *(citizen of Brussels, a tailor) steps forward and bends his crossbow.* SOEST *(citizen of Brussels, a shopkeeper)*

SOEST: Shoot away, and let's have it over with! You can't possibly take it from me now! Three rings inside the black—you never shot that in all your born days. That settles it, and I am Master this year.

JETTER: Master, and King on top of that! Who begrudges it to you? You'll have to take over a double share of the reckoning for it. You must pay for your skill—that's only fair.

BUYCK: *(a Hollander, soldier, serving under Egmont)* Jetter, let's strike a bargain: I'll take your shot for you, divide the prize, and treat the gentlemen. I've been here for some time now and am in debt for many civilities. If I miss, it will be just the same as if you had shot your turn yourself.

SOEST: I ought to object, for I'm the one who stands to lose by it. But go ahead, Buyck!

BUYCK: *(shoots)* Come on, now, marker! Count out your bows.—One! two! three! four!

SOEST: For rings inside the black? So be it!

ALL: Hail, King! Hurrah! Hurrah!

BUYCK: Thank you, gentlemen! "Master" would be too much! I thank you for the honor.

JETTER: You have only yourself to thank for it.

RUYSUM: (*a Friesland man, a disabled soldier. He is deaf.*) I must say—

SOEST: How goes it, old fellow?

RUYSUM: I must say he shoots like his master, he shoots like Egmont.

BUYCK: Compared with him, I'm a bungler. And with a musket he's a marksman like nobody in the world. I don't mean when he's lucky or in the vein. No, no—every time he aims, he hits the center. I learned from him. I'd like to see the man who could serve with him and not learn from him!—But I'm not forgetting, gentlemen. A King maintains his people—and so, at the King's expense, bring on the wine!

JETTER: It's always been understood among us that each man—

BUYCK: I am a foreigner and the King, and do not respect your laws and customs.

JETTER: Why, you're worse than the Spaniard. So far, even he has had to let us hold to them.

RUYSUM: What?

SOEST: (*loudly*) He wants to treat us. He won't let us contribute and leave the King to pay only a double share.

RUYSUM: Well, let him. But without making a precedent

of it. It's his master's way too, to be open-handed and spend freely where it will do good.

(*Wine is brought.*)

ALL: His Majesty's health! Hurrah!

JETTER: (*to* BUYCK) They mean *your* Majesty, of course.

BUYCK: I thank you heartily, if that is how it's to be.

SOEST: Good! For our Spanish Majesty's health is something that a Netherlander finds it hard to drink heartily.

RUYSUM: Who?

SOEST: (*loudly*) Philip the Second, King of Spain.

RUYSUM: Our most gracious Lord and King! God grant him long life!

SOEST: Didn't you like his father, Charles the Fifth, better?

RUYSUM: God keep him! That was a King! His hand covered the earth, he was everything and everywhere. Yet when he met you he greeted you like neighbor to neighbor; and if you were frightened, he had such a kindly way—you know what I mean—he rode out or walked out, just as he felt like it, with hardly any followers. Not a man of us but wept when he resigned the government here to his son—I mean, you know—*he's* very different, he's more august.

JETTER: While he was here he never showed himself except in full royal state. They say he speaks very little.

SOEST: He is no ruler for us Netherlanders. Our princes must be cheerful and genial like ourselves, live and let live. We won't stand for being looked down on or oppressed, goodhearted fools though we are.

JETTER: I think the King would be a gracious ruler, if only he had better councillors.

SOEST: No, no, he has no feeling for us Netherlanders, his heart is closed to the people, he does not love us; so how can we love him? Why is everyone so fond of Count Egmont? Why would we all wait on him hand and foot? Because it's plain to see that he likes us; because cheer and geniality and goodwill shine from his eyes, because there's not a thing of all he owns he wouldn't share with anyone in need or even not in need. Long live Count Egmont! Buyck, it is for you to propose the first health. Make it your master's!

BUYCK: With all my heart! I give you Count Egmont!

RUYSUM: Victor at St. Quentin!

BUYCK: The hero of Gravelines!

ALL: Long live Count Egmont!

RUYSUM: St. Quentin was my last battle. It was all I could do to get out at all, to say nothing of carrying a heavy musket. But I still managed to give the French something to remember. And by way of a goodbye I got one last grazing shot in my right leg.

BUYCK: Gravelines! What a day, my friends! And the victory was ours and nobody else's. The French dogs were burning and scorching their way all through Flanders. But I think we gave them what for! Their old stalwarts held out a long time, but we kept coming at them and firing and laying about us until they looked quite unhappy and their line began to sag. Just then Egmont's horse was shot dead under him, and we fought back and forth a long time, man to man, horse to horse, squad against squad, all over the broad level sands down to the sea. All of a sudden, as if out of the sky, *boom boom* from the mouth of the river—a stream of cannon-fire into the French. It was some of the English, who happened to be sailing past on their way from Dunkirk, under Admiral Malin. Actually, they didn't help us much —only their smallest ships could get in, and those not close enough; and some of their shot landed among us. Still, it did our hearts good! It broke the French and raised our courage. From then on, we had it all our own way. Biff, bang, up, down—we either shot them dead in their tracks or drove them into the water. The minute they hit the water they started to drown—and every Hollander of us in after them! Being amphibious, we took to it like frogs; and those that we didn't cut to pieces in the river, we shot down like ducks. A few managed to fight their way out of it, but it did them no good—you should have seen the peasant women knocking them dead with hoes and pitchforks as they tried to sneak away! And his French Majesty had to sit up on his little haunches like any lapdog and make peace then and there. And you owe that peace to us—to us and the great Egmont.

ALL: Hurrah for Egmont! Hurrah! Hurrah!

JETTER: If only they had made *him* regent over us instead of Margaret of Parma!

SOEST: No, no! Truth is truth. I won't hear a word against Margaret. Now it's my turn. Long live our gracious lady!

ALL: Long may she live!

SOEST: There are first-rate women in the royal house—nobody can deny *that*. Long live the Regent Margaret!

JETTER: She's a clever woman, and she keeps within bounds in everything she does. If only she weren't so hand in glove with the priests. After all, she is partly responsible for the fourteen new bishops they've saddled us with. And what are they for? What's behind it—I ask you—except that foreigners can be given the fat benefices, instead of abbots being elected from the chapters, as they used to be? And we're supposed to believe it's for religion's sake! Don't make me laugh! We had enough and plenty with three bishops; then everything went properly and decently. Now each of them has to act as if he's really needed; so there's constant trouble and bickering. And the more you look into it, the dirtier it gets. (*They drink.*)

SOEST: It was the King's will. She can do nothing about it one way or the other.

JETTER: And now we're forbidden to sing the new Psalms. And they have the prettiest rhymes and really heart-warming tunes. But we're not to sing them, though we can sing all the bawdy songs we please! And why? Because they say there are heresies in them and God knows what. Yet I've sung some of them myself—they're a change from the old ones—but I can't see anything wrong in them.

BUYCK: If I were you, I'd say something! In our Province we sing what we please. That's what comes of our having

Count Egmont for governor; he doesn't bother his head about such things. In Ghent, Ypres, all through Flanders, anybody sings them who wants to. (*loudly*) Can anything be more innocent than a hymn? Isn't that so, old fellow?

RUYSUM: Of course. It's a way of worshipping God, it's edifying.

JETTER: But *they* say it's not right—not what *they* call right. In any case, it's dangerous; so we let them alone. The agents of the Inquisition are on the prowl everywhere, watching, listening. Many a decent man has got into trouble already. Pressure on our consciences—that's the last straw! Since I'm not allowed to do what I want, they might at least let me go on thinking and singing what I please!

SOEST: The Inquisition will never get anywhere. We're not made like the Spaniards—we won't let our consciences be tyrannized over. The nobility should try to clip the Inquisitors' wings for them, before it's too late.

JETTER: It's a bad business. If these fellows take it into their heads to come rushing into my house, and there I am, sitting at my work, humming a French Psalm, without even thinking about it one way or the other, but just humming because the tune is in my head—I'm a heretic then and there, and they clap me into prison. Or suppose I'm walking along and stop by a group of people who are listening to a new preacher, one of the ones that have come here from Germany; I'm called a rebel on the spot and am in danger of losing my head. Did any of you ever hear one of them preach?

soest: They're good, honest men. I heard one not long ago, out in the fields, speaking to thousands and thousands of people. It was a very different kettle of fish from our preachers pounding away on the pulpit and choking the congregation with chunks of Latin. He spoke right out; he said they had been leading us all by the nose and keeping us stupid, and that now we could get more light. And, I tell you, he proved it all out of the Bible.

jetter: There must be something in it. I always said so, and I've thought about it a lot. It's been going around in my head for a long time.

buyck: Everybody is running to them, too.

soest: No wonder—since they can hear something good and something new.

jetter: And what if they do? After all, anyone ought to be allowed to preach as he has a mind to.

buyck: Look alive, gentlemen! With all this chatter you're forgetting the wine and Orange.

jetter: Let's never forget him! He's a real bulwark. When you think of him, you feel you could hide behind him and the Devil himself couldn't get at you there. Long live William of Orange!

all: William of Orange! Hurrah!

soest: And now, old fellow, it's your turn to give a toast.

ruysum: Old soldiers! *All* soldiers! Long live war!

BUYCK: Good for you, old man. Here's to all soldiers! Long live war!

JETTER: War, war! Do you know what you're asking for? Naturally, you soldiers have it on the tip of your tongue. But I can't tell you how it makes *our* hearts sink. To hear the drums beating all year long! To hear of nothing except how one troop is marching along here and another there; how they came over a slope and made a stand by a mill; how many were left lying on one field, and how many on another; and how they push on, and one side wins and the other loses, and nobody can ever make out who wins or loses what! How a town is taken and the men killed, and what happens to the poor women and innocent children! Nothing but misery and anxiety and thinking every minute, "They're coming! It's our turn this time."

SOEST: That's why a citizen must always be drilled in arms.

JETTER: And that's just what everyone who has a wife and children does. Yet I'd rather hear about soldiers than see them.

BUYCK: I ought to take offense at that.

JETTER: I didn't mean you, countryman. Once we got rid of the Spanish garrisons, we could breathe again.

SOEST: They did bear down on *you*, didn't they?

JETTER: Mind your own business!

SOEST: That was a sharp lot they had billeted in your house.

JETTER: Hold your tongue!

SOEST: They'd driven him out of the kitchen, the cellar, the parlor—out of bed. (*They laugh.*)

JETTER: You're a fool.

BUYCK: Peace, gentlemen! Must the soldier cry "Peace"? Well, since you have no liking for us, propose your own toast, a real citizen's toast.

JETTER: That we will! Security and Peace!

SOEST: Order and Freedom!

BUYCK: Excellent! We're all in favor of that too. (*They clink glasses and gaily repeat the words, but each calling out a different one, so that the result is a sort of round. Old Ruysum listens, and finally joins in too.*)

ALL: Security and Peace! Order and Freedom!

SCENE TWO

Palace of the REGENT MARGARET. MARGARET OF PARMA *in hunting dress. Courtiers, Pages, Servants.*

MARGARET: There will be no hunt, I do not wish to ride today. Tell Machiavelli to come here to me.
(*Exeunt all but* MARGARET)
The thought of these dreadful events leaves me no peace! Nothing can divert me, nothing distract me; the same scenes are ever before me, bringing the same anxieties. The King will now say this is what comes of my kindness, my leniency. Yet my conscience keeps telling me that I have done what is wisest and best. Was I to give way to

anger that, like a stormwind, would but have roused and
spread these flames all the sooner? I hoped to contain
them, to bank them in themselves. Ah, yes—what I tell
myself, what I well know, excuses me in my own eyes.
But how will my brother regard it? For there is no denying
it—the arrogance of the foreign preachers has increased
every day. They have blasphemed our sacred religion, con-
fused the stupid minds of the people, deluded them, put
them under a spell. Impious elements have mingled with
the rioters, and things have happened so dreadful that the
mind shudders to think of them—things that I must now
hasten to report to the court in detail, lest the King think
that more is being concealed from him. I see no way: neither severity nor mildness will halt the evil now. Oh, what
are we, the great, on the tide of humanity? We believe
that we control it, and it tosses us up and down, hither
and thither.

(*Enter* MACHIAVELLI.)

MARGARET: Are the letters to the King prepared?

MACHIAVELLI: They will be ready for you to sign in an
hour.

MARGARET: Have you made the report sufficiently full?

MACHIAVELLI: Full and circumstantial, as the King likes
a report to be. I describe how the iconoclastic frenzy first
showed itself in the countryside around St. Omer; how a
raging mob, carrying staves, axes, hammers, ladders, ropes,
yet escorted by only a few armed men, attacked chapels,
churches, monasteries and convents, drove away the wor-

shippers, forced open locked doors, turned everything up-
side down, tore down altars, smashed the images of the
saints, destroyed every painting, broke, ripped to pieces,
trampled on everything sacred or consecrated that they
came upon. I tell how the mob grew as they advanced,
how the inhabitants of Ypres opened the city gates to
them; how in an unbelievably short time they sacked the
cathedral, then burned the Bishop's library. How an immense mob of people, seized by the same madness, swarmed
through Menin, Comines, Wervicq, Lille, nowhere meeting any resistance; and how the monstrous conspiracy declared itself and accomplished its purpose at the very
same moment almost throughout Flanders.

MARGARET: Ah, how the anguish of it comes over me
again as you recount it! And fear, too, that the evil will
only increase! Tell me what you think, Machiavelli.

MACHIAVELLI: If Your Highness will forgive me, my
thoughts look decidedly black. And even though Your
Highness has always been pleased with my services, you
have seldom deigned to follow my advice. You have often
said playfully, "You see too far, Machiavelli. You should
be a historian; those who act can be concerned only with
the next step." And yet, did I not prophesy this? Did I
not foresee it all?

MARGARET: I too foresee much, but cannot change it.

MACHIAVELLI: To put it in the fewest possible words:
you cannot suppress the new doctrine. So give it legal
status, separate these people from the orthodox believers,

give them churches, assign them a place in the structure
of society, contain them; by these means you will quiet
the rioters at once. Any other procedure is futile, and you
will ruin the country.

MARGARET: Have you forgotten the horror with which
my brother himself dismissed the suggestion of tolerating
the new doctrine? Do you not know how zealously he ad-
vises me in every letter to uphold the true faith? That he
will not hear of restoring peace and unity at the expense
of our religion? Does he not keep his own spies, unknown
to us, throughout the Provinces, in order to learn who
shows any inclination to the new way of thinking? Has
he not amazed us by naming first one, then another in our
very entourage who has been secretly guilty of heresy?
Has he not ordered us to be severe and merciless? And I
am to be mild? I am to suggest conciliation, toleration to
him? Should I not lose all his confidence and faith in
me?

MACHIAVELLI: I am well aware that the King gives orders, that he communicates his intentions to you. He would
have you restore quiet and peace by a policy that makes
the people even more embittered, that will inevitably kindle
war from one end of the country to the other. Consider
what you are doing. The most important merchants have
caught the infection, the nobility, the people, the soldiery.
What use is it to cling to our views when everything is
changing around us? If only some good angel would put it
into Philip's head that it is more honorable for a king to

rule over citizens of two creeds than drive them to mutual extermination!

MARGARET: Never say such a thing again! I know well that politics can seldom keep faith, that it banishes all frankness, kindliness, forbearance from our hearts. In worldly affairs, all this is only too true, alas! But shall we deal with God as we do among ourselves? Are we to be indifferent to our well-tried belief, for which so many have given their lives? Would you have us sacrifice it to strange, uncertain, self-contradictory innovations?

MACHIAVELLI: Think not the worse of me for this, I beg you.

MARGARET: I know you and your loyalty. And I know that a man can be honorable and wise, even though he has missed the nearest and best way to his soul's salvation. There are other men too, Machiavelli, whom I value and yet must censure.

MACHIAVELLI: To whom do you refer?

MARGARET: I must admit that Egmont displeased me profoundly today.

MACHIAVELLI: By doing what?

MARGARET: By his usual attitude—his indifference and frivolity. I received this dreadful news as I was coming out of church, attended by many, among them himself. I did not conceal my distress, I spoke it aloud, and, turning to him, cried, "See what things are coming to in your province! Do you tolerate this, Count—you of whom the King expected everything?"

MACHIAVELLI: And what was his answer?

MARGARET: As if it were nothing at all, the merest incident, he retorted, "If the Netherlanders were once assured of their constitution, the rest would follow of itself."

MACHIAVELLI: Perhaps there was more truth than wisdom and piety in what he said. How can trust arise and endure when the Netherlander sees that his possessions are of more concern than his welfare or the salvation of his soul? Have the new bishops saved more souls than they have swallowed fat benefices? And are not most of them foreigners? At present all the governorships are still filled by Netherlanders, but do not the Spaniards let it be seen only too clearly that they have an overpowering hunger for those posts? Does not any people prefer to be governed in its own way by rulers of its own blood than by foreigners whose first concern as newcomers is to acquire possessions in the country at everyone's expense, who bring foreign standards with them, and govern without grace and without sympathy?

MARGARET: You take our opponents' side.

MACHIAVELLI: Certainly not with my feelings. And I would that I could be entirely on our side with my reason.

MARGARET: If that is your view, I should have to resign my regency to them. For Egmont and Orange had the greatest hopes of filling the post. At that time they were rivals; now they are allies against me; they have become friends, inseparable friends.

MACHIAVELLI: A dangerous pair.

MARGARET: To speak frankly, I fear Orange and I fear for Egmont. Orange is up to no good; his thoughts go very far, he is sly, he appears to accept everything, never raises an objection, and with the deepest respect he most discreetly does exactly as he pleases.

MACHIAVELLI: Egmont is just the opposite: he strides ahead as if the world belonged to him.

MARGARET: He carries his head as high as if the King's hand were not over him.

MACHIAVELLI: The people all keep their eyes on him, and their hearts are his.

MARGARET: He has never considered what impression he may make, as if he were answerable to no one. He still keeps the name Egmont. To hear himself called Count Egmont delights him; it is as if he had no wish to forget that his ancestors held Gelderland. Why does he not call himself Prince of Gavre, as he should? What is his purpose? Does he hope to revive extinct claims?

MACHIAVELLI: I consider him a faithful servant of the King.

MARGARET: If he only would, how useful he could make himself to the government! Instead, he has already caused us unspeakable trouble, without the least advantage to himself. His receptions, banquets, and carousals have done more to bring and keep the nobility together than the most dangerous secret meetings. What with drinking the toasts he keeps proposing, his guests work themselves into a state of perpetual intoxication, of never-diminishing delusion. How often his jesting words have stirred up the country, and what a sensation the new servants' liveries with their ridiculous emblems are causing among the mob!

MACHIAVELLI: I am convinced that it was not intentional.

MARGARET: So much the worse. As I said, he hurts us without benefiting himself. He trifles over things that are serious. And we, in order not to appear inactive and negligent, have to be serious over trifles. So one thing follows another—and what we try to avoid is precisely what happens. He is more dangerous than any determined leader of a conspiracy, and if I am not completely mistaken the Court takes note of everything he does. I cannot but say that he almost constantly annoys me, annoys me deeply.

MACHIAVELLI: It seems to me that in everything he does he acts according to his conscience.

MARGARET: Then his conscience has a highly accommodating mirror. His behavior is frequently offensive. He often gives the impression of being completely convinced that he is the master, of merely being too polite to let us feel it, of not quite wanting to drive us out of the country here and now, since it's bound to happen in due course in any event.

MACHIAVELLI: I beg you not to put such a dangerous interpretation on his frankness, his happy-go-lucky nature, which takes everything serious lightly. You merely injure him and yourself.

MARGARET: I am interpreting nothing. I am merely stating the inevitable consequences, and I know him. His

Netherlandish nobility and the Golden Fleece he displays on his chest strengthen his confidence, his boldness. Both can protect him against any sudden arbitrary displeasure of the King. Search to the root of it and you will see that he alone is guilty of all the misfortunes from which Flanders is suffering. First of all, he was indulgent with the foreign preachers, considered it nothing to make a fuss over, and was perhaps secretly glad that it gave us something to worry about. Let me do this in my own way! I have much on my mind, and I take this opportunity of putting it into words. And I shall not shoot my arrows in vain; I know where he is sensitive. He too has sensibilities.

MACHIAVELLI: Have you had the council summoned? Is Orange to attend too?

MARGARET: I have sent to Antwerp for him. I shall put the burden of responsibility on them, right enough. Either they shall join with me in taking serious measures against the evil, or they shall declare themselves rebels. Now get the letters ready as quickly as possible, and bring them to me to sign. Then send the trusty Vasca to Madrid. He is tireless and loyal; let him see to it that my brother receives the news from him first, before any rumor reaches him. I will speak with him myself before he leaves.

MACHIAVELLI: Your orders shall be promptly and duly executed.

SCENE THREE

A Citizen's House. CLARA, CLARA'S MOTHER, BRACKENBURG

CLARA: Won't you hold my yarn for me, Brackenburg?

BRACKENBURG: Please excuse me, Clara dear.

CLARA: What is troubling you this time? Why do you deny me this little service?

BRACKENBURG: Your thread fixes me to the spot before you, I cannot escape your eyes.

CLARA: Nonsense! Come here and hold it.

MOTHER: (*in an armchair, knitting*) Come, why don't you sing a song? Brackenburg sings such a pretty second to you. You used to be gay, and I always had something to laugh about.

BRACKENBURG: Used to be . . .

CLARA: Very well, we'll sing.

BRACKENBURG: As you please.

CLARA: But cheerily and don't drag! It's a little soldier's song, my favorite.

(*She winds yarn and sings with* BRACKENBURG.)

Strike up the drum!
Sound the fife!
My lover, armed,
Commands the troop,
Holds high his lance,
And all obey.
How my heart beats!
How my blood boils!
Oh, had I a doublet
And hose and a hat!

I'd follow him out the gate,
Striding boldly along,
Go through the Provinces,
Go everywhere.
The enemy give ground,
We pour in our fire.
No joy can compare
With being a man!

(*While they sing,* BRACKENBURG *frequently looks at* CLARA; *finally his voice fails him, tears come into his eyes, he lets the skein drop and goes to the window.* CLARA *finishes the song alone, her mother motions to her half reproachfully, she rises, goes a few steps toward* BRACKENBURG, *then turns irresolutely and sits down again.*)

MOTHER: What's happening in the street, Brackenburg? I hear marching.

BRACKENBURG: It's the Regent's body-guard.

CLARA: At this hour? What can that mean? (*She rises, goes to the window, and stands beside* BRACKENBURG.) That is not the regular day guard; there are many more of them! Almost all their troops! O, Brackenburg, go and listen, find out what's happening. It must be something out of the ordinary. Go, dear Brackenburg, do me the favor!

BRACKENBURG: I'm off. I'll be back directly. (*He holds out his hand to her as he leaves; she gives him hers.*)

MOTHER: You send him away so soon?

CLARA: I am curious. And besides—don't hold it against me—his presence makes me unhappy. I never know how I ought to behave toward him. I am wronging him, and it preys on my mind that he feels it so deeply. But there's nothing I can do about it now!

MOTHER: He is such a loyal fellow.

CLARA: And I cannot stop treating him affectionately. My hand often responds unconsciously when his presses mine so gently, so lovingly. I reproach myself that I am deceiving him, that I am nourishing a vain hope in his heart. It's a difficult position for me. God knows, I am not deceiving him. I do not want him to hope, and yet I cannot condemn him to despair.

MOTHER: That is not good.

CLARA: I was fond of him, and I still wish him well with all my heart. I could have married him, though I think I was never in love with him.

MOTHER: Yet you would have been happy with him.

CLARA: I should have been provided for and have had an untroubled life.

MOTHER: And now you've deliberately thrown it all away.

CLARA: I am in a very strange situation. When I try to think how it has happened, I know and I don't know. And then I have only to see Egmont again, and I understand it all perfectly—indeed, I could understand much *more* than has happened. Oh, what a man he is! All the Provinces worship him—and when I am in his arms, should I not be the happiest creature in the world?

MOTHER: How will it be in the future?

CLARA: Oh, the only question I ask is—Does he love me?

And is there any question whether he loves me?

MOTHER: Children bring us nothing but anxiety. What will be the end of it! Nothing but worry and grief! It will come to no good. You have made yourself unhappy—and made me unhappy too!

CLARA: (*calmly*) You let it go on in the beginning.

MOTHER: Alas, I was too kind-hearted, I have always been too kind-hearted.

CLARA: When Egmont rode by and I ran to the window, did you scold me then? Didn't you come to the window yourself? When he looked up, smiled, nodded, greeted me, did you dislike it? Did you not consider that you yourself were honored in your daughter?

MOTHER: Go on—reproach me!

CLARA: (*touched*) And then when he passed through the street oftener, and we could not help feeling that he came this way for my sake, didn't you notice it yourself with secret delight? Did you call me away when I stood behind the window-pane waiting for him to pass?

MOTHER: Did I think that it would go so far?

CLARA: (*in a faltering voice and holding back her tears*) And then when he came one evening, wrapped in his cloak, and surprised us in the lamplight, who bustled about making him welcome, while I sat dazed as if chained to my chair?

MOTHER: And had I any reason to fear that this unfortunate love would so quickly carry away my level-headed little Clara? Now I must bear it that my daughter—

CLARA: (*bursting into tears*) Mother! How can you? You take pleasure in tormenting me!

MOTHER: (*crying*) That's right—cry! Make me even more wretched by your grief. Isn't it burden enough for me that my only daughter is an abandoned creature?

CLARA: (*rising, coldly*) Abandoned! Egmont's beloved abandoned? What princess would not envy poor Clara her place in his arms! O Mother, Mother—you did not use to say such things. Dear Mother, be kind—The people, the neighbors—what does it matter what such creatures think or mutter!—This room, this little house is a heaven since Egmont's love has dwelt in it.

MOTHER: It is impossible not to like him—that's the truth. He is always so friendly, so natural and frank.

CLARA: There's not a false drop of blood in him. And think, Mother—he is the great Egmont too. And when he comes to me, how sweet he is, how kind! How much he would like to hide his rank, his heroism, from me! How preoccupied with me he is!—so completely and only the human being, the friend, the lover.

MOTHER: He's coming today, I suppose?

CLARA: Haven't you seen me keep going to the window? Haven't you noticed how I listen when there's a noise at the door? Even though I know that he won't come before nightfall, I expect him every minute, from the time I wake in the morning. If only I were a boy and could be with him always, go to Court and everywhere with him! If I could follow him in battle, carrying his banner!—

MOTHER: You were always so changeable, even when you were a little girl—all on fire one minute and lost in thought the next. Aren't you going to dress up a little?

CLARA: Perhaps, Mother, if I get bored!—Just think, some of his men went by yesterday, singing songs in praise of him! At least his name was in the songs; I couldn't understand the rest. My heart was in my throat . . . I would have called them back, only I felt ashamed.

MOTHER: Be careful. Your impulsiveness will ruin everything yet. You give yourself completely away before people. You did it at your cousin's, when you came on that woodcut with the description and you cried out, "Count Egmont!" I blushed as red as fire.

CLARA: What could I do but cry out? It was the Battle of Gravelines. And I found "C" up above in the picture and looked for "C" underneath in the description. And there it was: "Count Egmont, whose horse was shot dead under him." It gave me gooseflesh all over—but then I had to laugh at the Egmont in the woodcut, as big as the tower of Gravelines right next to him and the English ships off on the side. I often think how I used to imagine a battle, and what kind of an idea I had of Count Egmont, when I was still a girl and people told about him, and of all the Counts and Princes—and how things are with me now! (*Enter* BRACKENBURG)

CLARA: What's happening?

BRACKENBURG: Nobody knows exactly. They say there has been disorder in Flanders recently and the Regent is afraid it may spread here. The castle is strongly garrisoned, there are countless citizens at the gates, and the mob are swarming in the streets.—I must hurry to my old father. (*He makes as if about to leave.*)

CLARA: Shall we see you tomorrow? I have to go and dress up a little. My cousin is coming and I look too slovenly. Come and help me for a minute, Mother. Take your book, Brackenburg, and bring me another story like it.

MOTHER: Good-bye.

BRACKENBURG: (*holding out his hand*) Your hand!

CLARA: (*avoiding giving him her hand*) Next time. (*Exeunt Mother and* CLARA.)

BRACKENBURG: (*alone*) I meant to leave again at once; and when she simply accepts it and lets me go, it almost drives me mad.—Wretch! does your country's fate leave you untouched, this growing disorder?—Are fellow countryman and Spaniard the same to you, and who shall rule and who is in the right?—How different I was when I was a schoolboy! When we were set an exercise, "Brutus' speech for Freedom, for practice in oratory," Fritz was always first, and the head-master would say, "If only it were in some sort of order, instead of all higgledy-piggledy." —In those days things were always at the boiling point, I felt an urgency.—Now I simply drag along after that girl's eyes. And yet I cannot leave her! And yet she cannot love me. No—she—she cannot have rejected me completely—— Not completely—yet half is as bad as nothing!—I will bear it no longer!——Can it be true, what a friend whispered to me only the other day—that she secretly receives a man at night, and that is why she always virtuously turns me out of the house before dark? No, it is not true, it is a lie, an infamous, slanderous lie! My Clara is as innocent as I am unhappy.—She has rejected me, cast me out of her heart ——And shall I go on living thus? I will not, will not bear it.——Already my country is increasingly torn by internal strife, and shall I simply let myself waste away while stirring things are doing? I will not bear it.—When the trumpet rings out, a shot sounds, I feel it to the marrow. Yet, ah, it does not rouse me, it does not summon me to play a part too, to help save my country, to dare all.—Miserable, shameful state! Better that I end it altogether. Not long ago, I threw myself into the water, I sank—but terrified nature was the stronger; I felt that I could swim, and saved myself against my will.——Could I only forget the time when she loved me, seemed to love me!—Why did that happiness penetrate to my very marrow? Why have these hopes dissipated all my joy in life, showing me a paradise from far off?—And that first kiss! that only kiss! We were here (*putting his hand on the table*), here alone—she had always been pleasant and friendly to me—then she seemed to soften—she looked at me—my mind, my senses whirled, and I felt her lips on mine.—And—and now?——Die, wretch! Why do you hesitate? (*He draws a vial from his pocket.*) I shall not have stolen you from my brother's medicine-chest in vain, O healing poison! You shall draw this net of fears and dizziness and mortal sweats yet more tightly about me, and so free me from it forever.

ACT II

SCENE ONE

A square in Brussels. JETTER *and a Master Carpenter meeting.*

CARPENTER: Didn't I tell you? I said a week ago at the guild that there would be trouble.

JETTER: Is it true, then, that they've plundered the churches in Flanders?

CARPENTER: They've gutted them—churches and chapels too. They've left nothing standing but the four bare walls. The scum of the earth! And our good cause suffers from it. We ought to have set forth our rights to the Regent before this happened, firmly and in proper order, and then stuck to them. If we speak now, if we assemble now, they'll say we are siding with the rebels.

JETTER: That's everyone's first thought: "What are you sticking your nose into it for? Where noses go, necks are not far behind."

CARPENTER: I am uneasy as soon as the mob begins to make trouble, the people that have nothing to lose. They make their pretext the same thing that *we* have to appeal to, and the country goes to ruin.

(SOEST *joins them.*)

27

SOEST: Good day, gentlemen! Anything new? It it true that the image-smashers are coming straight here?

CARPENTER: They shall not touch anything here.

SOEST: A soldier came into my shop to buy tobacco. I asked him about things. Not to say that the Regent isn't a brave and clever woman, but this time she doesn't know what to do. The situation must be very bad when she goes and hides behind her guard. The castle is garrisoned and on the alert. They're even saying she intends to flee the city.

CARPENTER: She shall not leave the city! Her presence protects us, and we will guard her better than her mustachioed Spaniards. And if she maintains our rights and privileges, we'll acclaim her.

(*A Soapmaker joins them.*)

SOAPMAKER: A nasty business! a bad business! There is unrest, and it will end in trouble.—Mind you hold your tongues, so you won't be taken for rebels too!

SOEST: We have with us the Seven Sages of Greece!

SOAPMAKER: I know there are many who secretly side with the Calvinists, who slander the bishops, and do not fear the King. But a loyal subject, an upright Catholic— (*Little by little a crowd gathers around them and listens.* VANSEN *joins them.*)

VANSEN: God give you good day, gentlemen. What is new?

CARPENTER: Don't have anything to do with him, he's a bad egg.

JETTER: Isn't he Doctor Wiets's clerk?

CARPENTER: By now he has had many masters. He was a clerk to begin with, but one master after another turned him away because of his knavery, so now he sneaks in and steals odd bits of business from the notaries and advocates, and he's a sot to boot.

(*More people enter and gather together in groups.*)

VANSEN: I see you're all here with your heads together. Well, it's worth talking about.

SOEST: I think so too.

VANSEN: Now if only some of us had courage and some of us had brains, we could break our Spanish chains at a stroke.

SOEST: Lord! That's no way to talk! We have taken an oath to the King.

VANSEN: And so has the King to us. Mark that.

JETTER: There's something in that. Say what you have in mind.

SOME OF THE OTHERS: Listen! he knows what he's talking about. He knows all the tricks.

VANSEN: I had an old master once, he had parchments and charters of ancient grants and contracts and immunities; he liked nothing so much as the rarest books. One of them had our whole constitution in it—how at first we Netherlanders were ruled by separate princes, all in accordance with traditional rights, privileges, and customs; how our ancestors had every respect for their prince when he ruled them as he should; and how they were on their guard as soon as he wanted to hew over the line. The

Estates stepped in at once—for every Province, no matter how small, had its Estates, its own Diet.

CARPENTER: Hold your tongue! That's an old story. Every decent citizen knows as much about the Constitution as he needs to.

JETTER: Let him talk. There's always something more to learn.

SOEST: He's perfectly right.

SEVERAL VOICES: Go on, go on! We don't hear the like of this every day.

VANSEN: That's just the way you of the citizen class are. You live from one day to the next, and as you inherited your businesses from your parents, so you let the government do whatever it pleases with you. You never inquire into the origin, the history, the rights of a ruler. And what with this negligence of yours, the Spaniards have got you in their net.

SOEST: Who thinks of such things? If only we have our daily bread!

JETTER: Damnation! Why didn't someone come forward and tell us all this in time?

VANSEN: I'm telling you now! The King in Spain, though luck has made him owner of all the Provinces, has no business ruling them any differently from the lesser princes who used to own them individually. Do you understand that?

JETTER: Explain it to us.

VANSEN: It's as clear as daylight. Don't you have to be

governed in accordance with the law of the land? And why is that?

A CITIZEN: True enough!

VANSEN: Doesn't the man from Brussels have a different law from the man from Antwerp? The man from Antwerp from the man from Ghent? And why is that?

OTHER CITIZENS: By God!

VANSEN: But if you let things go on as they're going, you'll soon be hearing a different tune. Faugh! What Charles the Bold and Frederick the Warrior and Charles the Fifth couldn't do, Philip now does through a woman.

SOEST: Right you are! The old princes tried it too in their time.

VANSEN: Of course! But our ancestors were on their guard. Whenever they took a dislike to an overlord, they'd take his son and heir away from him, for example, and keep him safe, and only let him go on the best of conditions. Our ancestors were men! They knew what was good for them! They knew how to go after a thing and get it done! Real men! And that's just why our privileges are so clear, our freedoms so well secured.

SOAPMAKER: What do you mean—freedoms?

THE PEOPLE: Our freedoms, our privileges! Tell us more about our privileges!

VANSEN: Though all the Provinces have their own, we men of Brabant have the most and the best. I've read it all.

SOEST: Go on.

JETTER: Out with it.

A CITIZEN: Please speak.

VANSEN: First it is written: The Duke of Brabant shall be a good and loyal sovereign to us.

SOEST: "Good"? Does it say "good"?

JETTER: "Loyal"? Is that what is says?

VANSEN: Just as I've told you. He is under an obligation to us, as we are to him. Secondly: He shall use no force or capricious authority on us, or any show of the same, or permit the same to be used or shown in any manner.

JETTER: Excellent, excellent! Use no force.

SOEST: Or any show of the same.

ANOTHER VOICE: Or permit the same to be used or shown. That's the main point. No one is permitted, in any manner.

VANSEN: In so many words.

JETTER: Get us the book.

A CITIZEN: Yes, we must have it.

OTHERS: The book, the book!

ANOTHER: We'll go to the Regent with the book.

ANOTHER: You shall speak for us, learned Doctor.

SOAPMAKER: Oh, the fools!

OTHERS: Something more from the book!

SOAPMAKER: I'll knock his teeth down his throat if he says another word.

THE PEOPLE: Just let us see anyone try to hurt him! Tell us about the privileges. Have we more privileges?

VANSEN: Many more, and very good and wholesome they are. It says in the book: The sovereign shall neither advance nor increase the clergy without the consent of the nobility and the Diets. Mark that. Nor shall he change the constitution of the country.

SOEST: It that what it says?

VANSEN: I'll show it to you in writing, from two or three hundred years ago.

CITIZENS: And we tolerate the new Bishops? The nobility must protect us, we'll make trouble!

OTHERS: And we let the Inquisition frighten us to death?

VANSEN: It's your own fault.

THE PEOPLE: We still have Egmont! And Orange! They're looking after our welfare.

VANSEN: Your brothers in Flanders have begun the good work.

SOAPMAKER: You dog! (*He strikes him.*)

OTHERS: (*interpose and shout*) Are you a Spaniard too?

ANOTHER: What! This honorable man?

ANOTHER: What! This learned man?

(*They attack the Soapmaker.*)

CARPENTER: For Heaven's sake, peace!

(*Others join the affray.*)

CARPENTER: Citizens, what are you doing!

(*Boys whistle, throw stones, set on dogs. Citizens stand and gape. People come running, others walk leisurely up and down, others play all kinds of tricks, shout and cheer.*)

OTHERS: Freedom and Privileges! Privileges and Freedom!

(*Enter* EGMONT *with his train*)

EGMONT: Quiet! Quiet, good people! What is afoot? Quiet! Separate them!

CARPENTER: Worshipful Lord, you come like an angel from heaven. Quiet! Can't you see? It is Count Egmont! Honor to Count Egmont!

EGMONT: Here too? What are you about? Citizens against citizens! Does not even the near presence of our royal Regent restrain your folly? Disperse, go to your occupations. It is a bad sign when you make holiday on working days. What happened?

(*The tumult gradually subsides, and all stand around him.*)

CARPENTER: They were fighting over their privileges.

EGMONT: Which they will yet irresponsibly destroy.— And who are you? You look like respectable people.

CARPENTER: We try to be so.

EGMONT: What is your trade?

CARPENTER: Carpenter and guild-master.

EGMONT: And you?

SOEST: Shopkeeper.

EGMONT: You?

JETTER: Tailor.

EGMONT: I remember you, you worked on the liveries for my people. Your name is Jetter.

JETTER: It is a great honor that Your Excellency should remember it.

EGMONT: I do not easily forget anyone I have once seen and talked with.—Whatever you people can do to keep the peace, do it; you have too many black marks against you as it is. Stop irritating the King; after all, the power is in his hands. A decent citizen, who earns his living honorably and diligently, has all the freedom he needs anywhere.

CARPENTER: True enough. But that is just the trouble. The idlers, the tosspots, the sluggards—saving your Excellency's presence, they raise a stink from sheer boredom and go scraping up privileges because they're hungry, and stuff the curious and credulous with any lies; to get someone to buy them a pot of beer, they start disturbances that will make thousands miserable. That's just what they want. We keep our houses and our strong-boxes too well guarded; they'd be only too glad to drive us from them with firebrands.

EGMONT: You shall have every assistance; measures have been taken to meet the evil energetically. Stand firm against the foreign doctrine, and do not deceive yourselves into thinking that privileges can be protected by insurrection. Stay in your houses; see to it that there is no assembling in the streets. Reasonable people can accomplish a great deal.

(*Meanwhile the greater part of the crowd has dispersed.*)

CARPENTER: We thank Your Excellency. Our thanks for your good words. Whatever lies in our power! (*Exit* EGMONT) A gracious lord! the true Netherlander! Nothing Spanish about him.

JETTER: If we only had him for our regent! It's a pleasure to obey him.

SOEST: The King takes good care to avoid that. He always fills the office with his own people.

JETTER: Did you notice his clothes? In the latest style, after the Spanish cut.

CARPENTER: A handsome gentleman.

JETTER: His neck would make a nice tidbit for a headsman.

SOEST: Are you mad? What are you thinking of?

JETTER: A stupid idea to come into one's head. But that's how I am. When I see a fine, long neck, I can't help thinking it's just right for beheading. Those damned executions —a man can't get them out of his mind. When the boys are in swimming, and I see a naked back, I instantly think of dozens of backs that I've seen whipped with rods. If I run into a good fat belly, I think I already see it grilling at the stake. At night in dreams I'm tortured in every limb; there's not a carefree hour left. I've almost forgotten what fun and merriment are; those fearful sights seem branded into my brain.

SCENE TWO

EGMONT'S *Residence. Secretary (at a table with papers. He rises restlessly.)*

SECRETARY: Still not here! and I've been waiting for him two hours, pen in hand, papers ready; and today I particularly wanted to get away early. I itch to go. I can hardly keep myself here, my impatience is so great. "Be punctual," he ordered me, just as he left—and now he doesn't come. There is so much to do, I shall not be finished before midnight. It's true that he rather looks the other way when something is wrong. But I should prefer it if he were stricter and would let me get away at the regular time. Then I should know where I stood. He certainly left the Regent a good two hours ago. Heaven knows whom he may have got involved with on the way.

(*enter* EGMONT)

SECRETARY: I am ready, and there are three messengers waiting.

EGMONT: I see I stayed away too long for you—you look annoyed.

SECRETARY: In accordance with your orders, I have been waiting for some little time. Here are the documents.

EGMONT: Donna Elvira will be angry with me when she learns that I detained you.

SECRETARY: You are pleased to jest.

EGMONT: No, no. You've nothing to be ashamed of. You show excellent taste. She's pretty; and it suits me very well that you have a friend in the castle. What do the letters say?

SECRETARY: A great deal; and little of it pleasant.

EGMONT: All the better that we have pleasures at home, so we needn't look for them from abroad. Many letters?

SECRETARY: More than enough, and there are three messengers waiting.

EGMONT: Speak up—what is most pressing?

SECRETARY: It is all pressing.

EGMONT: Well then, in order—but quickly.

SECRETARY: Captain Breda submits his report of further occurrences in Ghent and the surrounding districts. The disorder has largely died down.—

EGMONT: No doubt he still reports individual cases of insolence and foolhardiness.

SECRETARY: Oh, yes. Such things are still happening.

EGMONT: Spare me the details.

SECRETARY: Six more of those who were involved in tearing down the image of the Virgin have been arrested. He asks if he shall have them hanged like the others.

EGMONT: I am tired of hangings. Let them be flogged and then released.

SECRETARY: Two of them are women. Are they to be flogged too?

EGMONT: He may warn them and let them go.

SECRETARY: Brink, of Breda's company, wants to marry. The Captain hopes that you will refuse him permission. There are so many women with the troops, he writes, that when we march off it will look more like a gypsy caravan than a company of soldiers.

EGMONT: Let it pass in Brink's case. He's a fine young fellow; he asked me most earnestly just before I left. But no more permissions to marry after his—much as I dislike denying the poor devils their best amusement, they have discomforts enough as it is.

SECRETARY: Two of your men, Seter and Hart, have mistreated a girl, an inn-keeper's daughter. They found her alone, and the wench could not defend herself against them.

EGMONT: If she was a respectable girl and they used force, he shall have them flogged with the rod three days in succession; and if they own anything, let him take as much of it as is necessary to provide the girl with a decent dowry.

SECRETARY: One of the foreign teachers has been caught trying to pass through Comines secretly. He swears he was leaving for France. By the regulation, he should be beheaded.

EGMONT: Let him be taken to the border quietly and told that if he tries it again he will not get off so easily.

SECRETARY: A letter has arrived from your steward. He writes that very little money is coming in; he can hardly send the sum you demanded within the week; the disturbances have put everything in the greatest confusion.

EGMONT: The money must be sent; it is for him to find a way to get it together.

SECRETARY: He says he will do his utmost and that he considers it high time to bring an action against Raymond, who has owed you money for so long, and have him arrested.

EGMONT: But he's already promised to pay.

SECRETARY: The last time he himself set a term of two weeks.

EGMONT: Then let him have another two weeks, and after that the steward can institute proceedings against him.

SECRETARY: An excellent solution. It is not that he is unable to pay; he just does not want to. He will certainly get down to business when he sees that you are in earnest.— Further from your steward: In regard to the old soldiers, the widows, and some others whom you pension, he wants to hold back their allowances for half a month; that will allow time for ways and means to be found; the pensioners must manage as they can.

EGMONT: How can they possibly manage? These people need the money more than I do. Tell him I won't hear of it.

SECRETARY: Then where is it your pleasure that he should turn for the money?

EGMONT: That is for *him* to consider; he was told as much in my last letter.

SECRETARY: And that is why he makes these proposals.

EGMONT: They won't do. Let him think of something else. Let him make proposals that are acceptable. And above all let him find the money.

SECRETARY: I have Count Oliva's letter here again. Excuse me for reminding you of it. The old gentleman deserves a full reply, if anyone does. You were going to write to him yourself. There is no doubt that he loves you like a father.

EGMONT. I have not time. And of all the things I dislike, writing letters is what I dislike most. You imitate my hand so well—write in my name. I am expecting Orange. I have not time; yet I should like to have something soothing written to him in answer to his fears.

SECRETARY: If you will just give me some idea of what you wish to have said, I will compose an answer at once and submit it to you. The hand shall be so like yours that it would pass as yours in court.

EGMONT: Give me his letter. (*after glancing through it*) Good, honorable old man! Could you have been as cautious when *you* were young as you are now? Did you never storm a rampart? In battle, did you always stay where wisdom counsels—at the rear? What devotion! what solicitude! He wants me to live and to be happy—and does not feel that anyone who lives for his own safety's sake is dead already.— Write to him, tell him not to worry. I act as I have to, I know how to take care of myself; if he wishes to use his influence at court in my favor, let him do so and be sure of my deepest gratitude.

SECRETARY: Is that all? He expects more.

EGMONT: What more am I to say? If you want to put it in more words, you are free to do so. It always comes back to one thing—he wants me to live as I cannot live. Being cheerful, taking things lightly, living fast is what makes my happiness; and I have no intention of exchanging it for the safety of a tomb. Not one drop of blood in my veins has any sympathy for the Spanish way of life, I have not the slightest wish to fit my steps to the new, cautious tune they are dancing to at court. Do I live only to think about life?

Shall I deny myself enjoying the present moment, in order to make sure of the moment to come? And then waste that on worry and bogies?

SECRETARY: I beg you, Sir, not to be so unyielding, so unkind with the good old man. You are always friendly with everyone else. Just give me a pleasant word or two, something that will reassure your noble friend. Observe how carefully he approaches you, with what a delicate touch—

EGMONT: Yet he always touches the same string. He has long known how I loathe all these admonitions; they only confuse things, they do no good. And if I were a sleep-walker, taking a dangerous stroll along the rooftree of a house, would it be an act of friendship to call me by name and warn me, to wake me and kill me? Let each go his own way, and look after himself.

SECRETARY: It is becoming in you to be unconcerned; but those who know and love you—

EGMONT: (looking at the letter) Here he goes raking up the old gossip about what we did and said in sheer high spirits one convivial evening over our wine, and all the conclusions and inferences that were drawn and spread over the kingdom. Well, we had fools'-caps and cowls embroidered on our servants' sleeves, and later changed those absurd ornaments into sheaves of arrows—an even more dangerous symbol for all those who insist on reading meaning into what has no meaning. That folly and others of ours had their conception and their birth in a single merry moment. We were responsible for a group of noblemen appearing with beggar's wallets and under a self-imposed absurd name in order that this mock humility should recall the King to his duty; we were responsible—but what of it? Is a carnival joke instantly high treason? Are we to be grudged the scanty particolored rags that youthful high spirits and excited imagination can hang on the wretched nakedness of our lives? If you take life too seriously, what does it amount to? If morning does not wake us to new pleasures, if we have no enjoyment to look forward to in the evening, is it worth getting dressed and undressed? Does the sun shine for me today that I may reflect on what was over and done with yesterday? divine and determine what cannot be divined or determined—the ineluctible course of a future day? Spare me these reflections; we will leave them to scholars and courtiers. Let them strive and contrive, crawl their devious ways, get where they can, and sneak back with what they can.—If you can use any of all this, so long as your letter doesn't become a book, you are free to do so. The good old man takes everything too seriously. So a friend who has long held one's hand gives it one firmer clasp when he decides to let it go.

SECRETARY: You must forgive me! The man plodding on foot grows dizzy when he sees someone rattling along in a carriage.

EGMONT: Child, child! Say no more! As if lashed on by invisible spirits, the Sun-god's coursers of the times carry the light chariot of our destiny on in their headlong gallop;

and there is nothing we can do save, ready and bold, to grasp the reins and guide the wheels now left, now right, here from a rock, there from a plunge. Who knows where he is bound? Scarcely can he remember whence he came.

SECRETARY: My lord, my lord!

EGMONT: I stand high, and I can and must mount yet higher; hope is with me, and courage and strength. I have not yet attained the summit of my growth. And if once I reach the height, I shall stand firmly planted—not in fear. If I must fall, let it be a lightning-bolt, a hurricane, nay, even a misstep of my own making, that plunges me into the abyss; I shall lie there with many thousands more. Never, even for a trifling stake, have I disdained to die with my worthy fellows-in-arms. And shall I hesitate when the stake is all the freedom and all the value of life?

SECRETARY: O my lord! you know not what you say! God protect you!

EGMONT: Gather up your papers. Orange is coming. Finish what is most pressing, so the messengers can be gone before the gates are shut. The rest can wait. Leave the letter to the Count until tomorrow. Do not fail to visit Elvira, and give her my greetings.—Keep your ears open and find out how the Regent is feeling; I hear she is not well, though she conceals it. (*Exit* SECRETARY)

(*Enter* ORANGE)

EGMONT: Welcome, Orange. You seem not wholly at your ease?

ORANGE: What do you think of our interview with the Regent?

EGMONT: I found nothing unusual in the way she received us. I have seen her so more than once before. I thought she was not in the best of health.

ORANGE: Did you not notice that she was more reserved? First she pretended calm approval of our conduct in regard to the recent mob uprising, later she remarked that it would nevertheless be easy to present it in a false light, then she turned the conversation to deliver her usual discourse on how her kindness and friendliness to us Netherlanders had never been duly appreciated or received fitting acknowledgment, that nothing was in the way of reaching a satisfactory issue, that she foresaw the moment when she would be sick and tired of it all, and that the King would then have to resolve to take other measures. Did you hear all that?

EGMONT: Not all of it. I was thinking of something else. She is a woman, my dear Orange, and women are always hoping that everything and everybody will cuddle quietly under their soft yoke, that every Hercules will doff his lion's skin and join their spinning circle. Being peaceably inclined themselves, they would fain believe that the ferment that seizes a people, the storm that powerful rivals raise in conflict with one another could be allayed by a single soothing word and the most opposed elements be reconciled in placid harmony at their feet. That is how it is with her. And since she cannot achieve her wish, she has no alternative but to be peevish, to complain of ingratitude and imprudence, to threaten the most dire prospects for the future—among them, that she will leave the country.

ORANGE: Don't you think this time that she may execute her threat?

EGMONT: Never! How often have I not seen her ready to set off! In control of the state here, a veritable queen— do you think she will enjoy the monotony of insignificance at her brother's court? Going to Italy and drifting from one tedious family intrigue to another?

ORANGE: You think her incapable of such a step because you have seen her hesitate, have seen her draw back. Yet she has it in her. New circumstances will drive her to execute her long-deferred resolution. And suppose that she goes—and that then the King sends someone else?

EGMONT: Why, someone else would come and he, too, would find himself with his work cut out for him. He would arrive with great plans, projects, ideas for putting everything in order, mastering everything and holding everything together. And he would find himself having to deal with one trifle today and tomorrow with another; day after tomorrow some other difficulty would have cropped up; he would spend the first month making plans, the second in indignation over projects that had failed, and half a year worrying about a single province. Time will run short for him too, his head will swim, and things will go on just as before—so that, instead of sailing across great seas along a predetermined course, he can thank God if in this storm he manages to keep his ship off the rocks.

ORANGE: But suppose the King were induced to try an experiment?

EGMONT: What experiment?

ORANGE: Seeing how the body would get on without the head.

EGMONT: What?

ORANGE: Egmont, for many years all our circumstances have been of the greatest concern to me; it is as if I stood over a game of chess, and I consider no move of our opponent without significance. And as men of leisure with nothing better to do try to unravel the secrets of Nature with the utmost attention, so I consider it the duty and the calling of a Prince to know the views and policies of all parties. I have reason to fear an eruption. The King has long acted in accordance with certain principles; he sees that they are leading him nowhere—what more likely than that he should try to attain his ends in some other way?

EGMONT: I do not believe it. When a man reaches old age and has attempted so much and the world refuses to be brought to order, he must finally have had enough of it.

ORANGE: There is one thing he has not tried.

EGMONT: And what may that be?

ORANGE: To indulge the people and destroy the Princes.

EGMONT: How many have long feared just that! There is no occasion for apprehension.

ORANGE: It was apprehension once; little by little it became suspicion; of late it has grown into certainty.

EGMONT: Has the King any more loyal servants than we?

ORANGE: We serve him in our way; and among ourselves we can admit that we know quite well how to balance the King's rights against our own.

EGMONT: Who but does likewise? We submit to him and are ready to serve him in all that is his due.

ORANGE: But what if he should claim that *more* was due to him, and term disloyalty what we call standing up for our rights?

EGMONT: We shall know how to defend ourselves. Let him assemble the Knights of the Golden Fleece; we will submit ourselves to their judgment.

ORANGE: And what if the judgment should precede the investigation, punishment the judgment?

EGMONT: That would be an injustice of which Philip would never be guilty, and a piece of folly of which I do not believe him or his councillors capable.

ORANGE: And what if his present councillors *are* unjust and foolish?

EGMONT: No, Orange, it is impossible. Who would dare to lay a hand on us?—To arrest us would be a doomed and a fruitless undertaking. No, they do not dare hoist the banner of tyranny so high. The breeze that spread such news over the country would whip up an immense conflagration. And what could their purpose be? The King cannot judge and condemn alone—could they be planning to have us secretly assassinated?—They cannot have any such intention. One grim resolve would unite the whole people on the instant. Hatred and eternal separation from the Spanish name would declare themselves in violence.

ORANGE: But it would be over our graves that the flames would rage, and the blood of our enemies would flow in empty atonement. Let us consider, Egmont.

EGMONT: But how could they possibly do it?

ORANGE: Alba is on the way.

EGMONT: I do not believe it.

ORANGE: I know it.

EGMONT: The Regent showed no sign of knowing it.

ORANGE: Which only makes me all the more certain. She will defer to him. I know his bloodthirsty cruelty. And he is bringing an army with him.

EGMONT: To burden the Provinces again? The people will never put up with it.

ORANGE: The government will seize their leaders.

EGMONT: No, no!

ORANGE: Let each of us go to his own Province. There we can strengthen ourselves. Alba will not begin with open force.

EGMONT: Must we not greet him when he arrives?

ORANGE: We will put it off.

EGMONT: Suppose that, when he comes, he summons us in the King's name?

ORANGE: We will find subterfuges.

EGMONT: And if he presses the matter?

ORANGE: We will excuse ourselves.

EGMONT: And if he insists?

ORANGE: All the more reason not to go.

EGMONT: And so war is declared, and we are the rebels. Do not let your cleverness mislead you, Orange; I know it is not fear that makes you retreat. Consider this step.

ORANGE: I have considered it.

EGMONT: Consider, if you are wrong, for what you will be responsible: for the most ruinous war that has ever devastated a country. Your refusal would be the signal that would call the Provinces to arms at once, that would justify every atrocity for which Spain has ever sought to grasp at any pretext. What we have so long and laboriously kept under control, you will lash into the most dire disorder by a single gesture. Think of the cities, of the nobles, of the people, of commerce, farming, trade! And think of the destruction, think of the slaughter! The soldier sees his comrade fall beside him on the battlefield and is not troubled. But you will see the river carrying the corpses of citizens, children, girls toward you, and horror will possess you and you will no longer know whose cause you are defending, for those for whose freedom you took up the sword will be perishing before your eyes. And how shall you feel when you shall have to admit to yourself: I took up the sword for my own safety?

ORANGE: We are not private men, Egmont. If it is right that we sacrifice ourselves for thousands, it is no less right that we save our lives for thousands.

EGMONT: The man who saves his life must suspect himself forever after.

ORANGE: The man who knows himself can advance and retreat with equal confidence.

EGMONT: The evil that you fear will become certainty through your action.

ORANGE: It is both wise and brave to go to meet an unavoidable evil.

EGMONT: In a situation of such peril, the slightest hope must be taken into consideration.

ORANGE: We have no more room for even the most cautious step. The abyss lies at our very feet.

EGMONT: Is the King's favor so narrow a ground?

ORANGE: Not so narrow, but slippery.

EGMONT: By God, he is wronged! I cannot bear these unjust thoughts of him! He is Charles's son and incapable of any baseness.

ORANGE: What kings do is never base.

EGMONT: He should be better known.

ORANGE: The knowledge we have of him tells us not to await the outcome of a dangerous test.

EGMONT: No test is dangerous if one has the courage for it.

ORANGE: You let yourself be carried away, Egmont.

EGMONT: I can only see with my own eyes.

ORANGE: Would that this time you saw with mine! Friend, because you keep your eyes open, you believe that you see. *I* am going. *You* may wait for Alba to arrive, and

God be with you! Perhaps my refusal will save you. Perhaps the dragon will think that he is catching nothing if he cannot swallow us both at once. Perhaps he will delay, in order to carry out his intention the more surely; and perhaps meanwhile you will see the situation as it really is. But then, make all speed! Save yourself, save yourself!—Farewell. Let nothing escape your attention—how many troops he brings with him, how he garrisons the city, what powers the Regent retains, how ready your friends are. Let me have news——Egmont—

EGMONT: What?

ORANGE: (taking his hand) Be persuaded! Come with me!

EGMONT: What? Tears, Orange?

ORANGE: A man may weep for a lost friend.

EGMONT: You think me lost?

ORANGE: Yes, lost. Reflect! You have but a short respite left. Farewell! (Exit)

EGMONT: (alone) That others' thoughts can have such influence on us! It would never have occurred to me; and this man infects me with his anxiety.—Away!—It is a foreign drop in my blood. Kind Nature, cast it out of me! And these furrows of thought on my brow—yes, I know there is still one ever ready means to soothe them away.

ACT III

The Regent's Palace. MARGARET OF PARMA.

MARGARET: I should have foreseen it. Ha! When we toil on from day to day, we think that we are doing all that is humanly possible; and he who watches and gives orders from a distance believes that he is demanding no more than anyone could do.—Oh, kings!—I should not have believed this thing could trouble me so greatly. It is so beautiful to rule! And to abdicate?—I do not know how my father was able to do it; but I will do it too.

(MACHIAVELLI *appears stage rear.*)

MARGARET: Approach, Machiavelli. I am reflecting on my brother's letter.

MACHIAVELLI: May I know what it contains?

MARGARET: As much tender consideration for me as solicitude for his states. He praises the steadfastness, industry, and loyalty with which I have hitherto protected His Majesty's rights in these lands. He regrets that the unruly people give me so much trouble. He is so thoroughly convinced of the profundity of my insight, so extraordinarily satisfied with the wisdom of my conduct, that I should almost say

53

his letter is too perfectly composed to be a king's, to say nothing of a brother's.

MACHIAVELLI: It is not the first time that he has expressed his well-justified satisfaction to you.

MARGARET: But the first time that it is sheer rhetoric.

MACHIAVELLI: I do not understand.

MARGARET: You will.—For after this introduction, he goes on to suggest that without troops, without a small army in fact, I shall always cut a sorry figure here! We were wrong, he says, to withdraw our soldiers from the Provinces on the complaints of the inhabitants. A garrison, he maintains, that will lie heavy on the citizens' necks will prevent them from becoming unduly restive.

MACHIAVELLI: It would cause intense irritation.

MARGARET: The King suggests, however—do you hear?—he suggests that an able general, one who will waste no time listening to arguments, could very quickly set things to rights among the people and the nobility, the townsmen and the peasants; and he is therefore sending one such, together with a strong army—the Duke of Alba!

MACHIAVELLI: Alba!

MARGARET: Are you surprised?

MACHIAVELLI: You say, "He is sending." Surely it is rather, "He asks if he shall send"?

MARGARET: The King asks nothing; he is sending him.

MACHIAVELLI: Then you will have an experienced soldier in your service.

MARGARET: In my service? Say what you really think, Machiavelli.

MACHIAVELLI: I cannot wish to anticipate you.

MARGARET: But I can wish to dissimulate. It hurts me, hurts me deeply. I would far rather have my brother say what he thinks than sign formal epistles drawn up by a secretary of state.

MACHIAVELLI: Can't they see . . . ?

MARGARET: I know them backwards and forwards. They want to have everything swept and tidied up; and since they don't use the broom themselves, anyone who comes along with one in his hand has their entire confidence. Oh, I see it as if the King himself and all his council were pictured in that tapestry there!

MACHIAVELLI: So vividly?

MARGARET: Not a feature is missing. There are good men among them. The honorable Rodrigo, so experienced and so moderate, who does not aim too high and yet neglects nothing; the upright Alonso, the industrious Freneda, the reliable Las Vargas, and several others, who go along whenever the good party is gaining strength. But there sits the hollow-eyed Toledan with his iron brow and deep, blazing gaze, muttering between his teeth about the conciliatory nature of women, untimely concessions, and that though ladies can ride trained palfreys well enough, they make poor horse-breakers, and similar pleasantries which in times past I have been obliged to listen to from these political gentlemen.

MACHIAVELLI: You have picked out an excellent paint-pot for your picture.

MARGARET: Admit it, Machiavelli: among all the hues with which I could possibly paint, there is no color as yellow-brown, as gall-black as Alba's complexion and as the color with which *he* paints. To him, everyone is a blasphemer and guilty of lèse-majesté from the outset, for under that category they can all be instantly racked, impaled, quartered, and burned.—The good that I have done here looks like nothing from a distance, simply because it is good.—So he harps on every past prank, rakes up every disturbance that has been pacified; and the King has such a picture of mutiny, sedition, and audacity set before him that he imagines the people here are still at one another's throats, when we have long since forgotten some transient insolence of an ill-bred populace. So he works himself into a mood of heartfelt hate for the poor wretches, he sees them as abhorrent, not to say as beasts and monsters; he looks for fire and the sword, and supposes them the only way to control human beings.

MACHIAVELLI: You are too vehement, I think; you take the matter too seriously. Are you not still Regent?

MARGARET: I know what that means. He will bring instructions with him.—I am experienced enough in political affairs to understand how someone can be supplanted without being deprived of his office. To begin with, he will bring instructions that are vague and equivocal; he will obtrude himself, for he has the power; and if I protest, he will allege secret instructions; if I ask to see them, he will put me off; if I insist, he will show me a document that refers to something entirely different; and if that does not satisfy me, he will do neither more nor less than he would if I had said nothing.—Meanwhile, he will have done what I fear and have undone what I hoped.

MACHIAVELLI: I wish that I could contradict you.

MARGARET: What I have pacified by inexpressible patience, he will stir up again by sternness and cruelties; I shall see my work ruined before my eyes and, as if that were not enough, shall have to bear the blame for his faults.

MACHIAVELLI: Your Highness should wait and see.

MARGARET: I have enough control over myself to remain calm. Let him come. I will make way for him as graciously as possible, before he forces me to do it.

MACHIAVELLI: Is a step of such consequence to be taken so precipitately?

MARGARET: It is harder to do than you think. He who is accustomed to rule, to whom it has become second nature that the fate of thousands rests in his hands every day, steps down from the throne as into the grave. But better that than to linger like a ghost among the living and seek, with appearances that deceive no one, to maintain a position to which another has succeeded and now possesses and enjoys.

SCENE TWO

CLARA'S *House.* CLARA. *Her mother.*

MOTHER: Such love as Brackenburg's I have never seen; I thought it only existed in old romances.

CLARA: (*walking up and down the room and humming a song*)

> Only the heart
> That loves is happy.

MOTHER: He suspects your association with Egmont. Yet I believe that if you would treat him a little kindly, he would still marry you if you wanted.

CLARA: (*singing*)

> Joyous
> And grieving,
> Full of thought;
> Longing
> And suffering
> In hovering pain;
> Blissful as heaven,
> Mortally sad;
> Only the heart
> That loves is happy.

MOTHER: Enough of that jingle.

CLARA: Don't scold me for singing it; it is a song of power. Haven't I put a great child to sleep with it often enough?

MOTHER: There's nothing in your head except your love. If only you didn't forget everything for that one thing. I tell you, you should treat Brackenburg decently. He can still make you happy some day.

CLARA: He?

MOTHER: Yes, yes. The time will come!—You children have no eyes for the future, and no ears for our experience. Youth, the joy of love—it all ends, and a time comes when one thanks God if one has somewhere to crawl and hide.

CLARA: (*shudders, is silent for a moment, then starts up*) Mother, let the time come as death comes. To think of it beforehand is horrible! And if death comes—when we must— then—we will act as we can—Egmont! to be without you! — (*Weeping*) No, it is impossible, impossible.

(*Enter* EGMONT, *wearing a horseman's cloak, with his hat pulled down to hide his face.*)

EGMONT: Clara dearest!

CLARA: (*cries out; then, starting back*) Egmont! (*She hurries to him.*) Egmont! (*She embraces him and leans against him.*) O kind one, dear one, sweet one! Have you come? are you here?

EGMONT: Good evening, Mother.

MOTHER: God be with you, noble sir. My child has very nearly pined to death because you have stayed away so long; again she has spent the whole day talking and singing about you.

EGMONT: I hope you will give me some supper?

MOTHER: We do not deserve such honor. If only we had something.

CLARA: Of course we will. Don't concern yourself,

Mother; I have seen to it; I have something ready. Don't give me away.

MOTHER: There's little enough, I warrant.

CLARA: Just wait and see! And then, I think—when he is with me, I don't feel hungry at all, and so he shouldn't feel very hungry when I am with him.

EGMONT: Is that what you think?

(CLARA *stamps her foot and turns from him reluctantly.*)

EGMONT: What's the matter?

CLARA: You are so cold today! You haven't even given me a kiss. Why do you keep your arms wrapped in your cloak, like a swaddled baby? Soldiers should never have their arms bound, nor lovers either.

EGMONT: At times, darling, at times they should. When a soldier is waiting in ambush to trick the enemy, he pulls himself together, wraps his arms around himself, and mulls over his plan until it is ripe. And a lover—

MOTHER: Won't you sit down? And make yourself comfortable? I must go to the kitchen; my Clara thinks of nothing when you are here. You must put up with whatever it turns out to be.

EGMONT. Your kindness is the best sauce.

(*Exit* MOTHER)

CLARA: If that is so, what is my love?

EGMONT: Whatever you like.

CLARA: I dare you to find a comparison for it.

EGMONT: But first— (*He throws off his cloak and appears in a magnificent costume.*)

CLARA: Good Heavens!

EGMONT: Now my arms are free. (*He embraces her.*)

CLARA: Stop! You'll spoil your clothes. (*She steps back.*)
How magnificent! Now I don't dare touch you.

EGMONT: Are you pleased? I promised I'd come once in
Spanish court dress.

CLARA: It's been a long time since I stopped asking you.
I thought you didn't want to.—Oh, the Golden Fleece, too!

EGMONT: You see it at last.

CLARA: Did the Emperor himself hang it around your
neck?

EGMONT: Yes, child. And the chain and the badge confer
the noblest privileges on any man who wears them. No one
on earth has the right to judge my acts except the Grand
Master of the Order in conclave with the entire chapter of
Knights.

CLARA: Oh, you could let the whole world judge you!—
The velvet is too wonderful for words, and the passemen-
terie, and the embroidery!—I don't know where to begin.

EGMONT: Just look your fill.

CLARA: And the Golden Fleece. You told me the story of
it, and you said it was the symbol of everything great and
precious that is deserved and won by toil and effort. It is
very precious—I can compare it to your love.—I carry your
love in my heart, just as you—but from there on—

EGMONT: What do you mean?

CLARA: From there on the comparison doesn't hold.

EGMONT: Why not?

CLARA: I didn't win your love with toil and effort, I didn't deserve it.

EGMONT: It is different with love. You deserve it because you make no effort to gain it—and almost the only people who attain it are those who don't run after it.

CLARA: Did you learn that from your own experience? Did you make that proud statement about yourself?—you whom the whole people loves?

EGMONT: If only I had done something for them! if only I *could* do something for them! It is out of the goodness of their hearts that they love me.

CLARA: I suppose you were with the Regent today?

EGMONT: Yes.

CLARA: Are you on good terms with her?

EGMONT: Outwardly, at any rate. We are perfectly amiable and prepared to be helpful to each other.

CLARA: And at heart?

EGMONT: I like her. We each have our own objectives. But that doesn't matter. She is a woman of great capacity, she knows the people with whom she is dealing, and would see into things well enough, even if she were not so inclined to be suspicious. I keep her very busy, because she is always looking for secrets behind my actions, and I have no secrets.

CLARA: None at all?

EGMONT: Well, perhaps a mental reservation now and then. Every wine deposits lees in the cask in the course of time. In any case, Orange keeps her even better entertained, the task he sets her is never-ending. He has made himself the reputation of always being about something secret; and she is forever searching his forehead for what he may be thinking, and his steps for where he may be going.

CLARA: Does she dissemble?

EGMONT: She is the Regent—and you ask that?

CLARA: Forgive me. I meant, is she false-hearted?

EGMONT: No more and no less than anyone else who is determined to attain his ends.

CLARA: I could never manage in that world! But then she has a masculine spirit, she is a different sort of woman from us seamstresses and cooks. She is great, stout-hearted, determined.

EGMONT: Yes, when things are not too hot and heavy. But this time she is not quite sure of herself.

CLARA: What do you mean?

EGMONT: To complete the portrait, she has a slight mustache on her upper lip, and often suffers from gout. A real Amazon!

CLARA: A majestic woman. I should be afraid to enter her presence.

EGMONT: Yet you are not timid in other respects—so it would not be fear, but just girlish bashfulness.

(CLARA casts her eyes down, takes his hand, and leans against him.)

EGMONT: I understand you, dear girl! You can look up. (He kisses her eyes.)

CLARA: Let me be silent! Let me hold you. Let me look

into your eyes, find everything there—comfort and hope and joy and grief. (*She embraces him and gazes at him.*) Tell me! Speak! I do not understand. Are you Egmont? Count Egmont? the great Egmont who is so famous, about whom they write in the newspapers, to whom the Provinces cling?

EGMONT: No, dear Clara, that is not who I am.

CLARA: What do you mean?

EGMONT: Listen, Clara.—Let me sit down!—(*He sits, she kneels before him on a footstool, rests her arms on his lap, and looks at him.*) *That* Egmont is a bad-tempered, stiff, cold Egmont, who has to keep a firm grip on himself, put on now one expression, now another; harassed, misjudged, involved, while everyone thinks him light-hearted and gay; loved by a people that does not know what it wants; honored and praised by a mob with which nothing can be done; surrounded by friends to whom he cannot trust himself; watched by men who would use any means to get the better of him; working and striving, often to no purpose, usually without any reward—oh! how he fares and feels is better left unspoken! But *this* Egmont, my Clara, *this* Egmont is at peace, free to speak, happy, is loved and known by the best of hearts, which he too knows and presses to his own in perfect love and trust. (*Embraces her*) That is *your* Egmont!

CLARA: Let me die so! The world has no joys after this!

ACT IV

SCENE ONE

A Street. JETTER. Carpenter.

JETTER: Hey! Psst! Hey, neighbor, a word with you!

CARPENTER: Go your way and keep quiet.

JETTER: Only a word. Nothing new?

CARPENTER: Nothing—except that we're forbidden to talk about anything new.

JETTER: What?

CARPENTER: Stop over here by the house. Be careful! The Duke of Alba no sooner arrived than he issued an order that if two or three talk together in the street they are guilty of high treason without trial.

JETTER: Misery!

CARPENTER: Discussing state affairs is forbidden on pain of imprisonment for life.

JETTER: Oh, our freedom!

CARPENTER: And criticizing any act of the government is punishable by death.

JETTER: Oh, our heads!

CARPENTER: In addition, great rewards are offered to entice fathers, mothers, children, relatives, friends, and servants to report what goes on in the privacy of our houses to a court especially set up for the purpose.

JETTER: Let's go home.

CARPENTER: And those who obey are assured that they will suffer no harm in body, honor, or estate.

JETTER: There's graciousness for you! Didn't I become uneasy the moment the Duke entered the town? Ever since then I've felt as if the sky were draped in black crape and hung so low that a man had to stoop to keep from knocking his head against it.

CARPENTER: And how did you like his soldiers? They're a different kettle of fish from those we've been used to.

JETTER: Faugh! It chills one's heart to see a troop of them march down the street. Straight as ramrods, eyes fixed, all perfectly in step no matter how many they are. And when they're standing guard and you pass by one of them, it's as if he wanted to stare you through and through, and he looks so stiff and threatening that you think you see a martinet at every corner. They don't make me happy at all. Our militia were cheerful fellows, weren't they?—they took their little liberties, stood with their legs straddled out, wore their hats cocked over one ear, lived and let live. But these fellows are like machines with a devil sitting inside.

CARPENTER: If one of them shouted "Halt!" and aimed at you, do you think you'd halt?

JETTER: I'd drop down dead on the spot.

CARPENTER: Let's go home.

JETTER: No good will come of all this. Good-bye.

(*Enter* SOEST)

SOEST: Friends! Neighbors!

CARPENTER: Quiet! Let us go.

SOEST: Have you heard?

JETTER: Only too much!

SOEST: The Regent has gone.

JETTER: Then God have mercy on us!

CARPENTER: She was still one to help us.

SOEST: All of a sudden and secretly; she couldn't get on with the Duke. She sent word to the nobles that she would come back. But nobody believes it.

CARPENTER: God forgive the nobles for letting in this new scourge to our backs. They could have prevented it. Our privileges are gone.

JETTER: For God's sake don't mention privileges! I can already smell an execution morning; the sun refuses to come out, the fogs stink.

SOEST: Orange has gone too.

CARPENTER: Then we are utterly abandoned!

SOEST: Count Egmont is still here.

JETTER: Thank God! May all the saints strengthen him to do his best! He's the only one of them all who can accomplish anything.

(*Enter* VANSEN.)

VANSEN: So at last I find a few who haven't crawled into their holes!

JETTER: Do us the favor of moving on.

VANSEN: You're not too polite.

CARPENTER: This is no time for ceremony. Is your back itching again? Are you all healed up so soon?

VANSEN: Ask a soldier about his wounds! If I had cared anything about blows, I should never have amounted to anything as long as I lived.

JETTER: Next time it may be worse.

VANSEN: The coming storm puts a lamentable weakness in your limbs, it seems!

CARPENTER: *Your* limbs will soon be exercising themselves somewhere else if you don't keep your mouth shut.

VANSEN: Pitiful mice! in despair because the master of the house brings home a new cat! One cat is much the same as another; we shall still get on now as we did before, don't you worry.

CARPENTER: You're a scurrilous rogue.

VANSEN: So says Master Nincompoop!—Just leave it to the Duke! The old tomcat looks as if he'd swallowed devils instead of mice and couldn't digest them. Just give him time; he has to eat and drink and sleep too, like everyone else. I'm not afraid, if we bide our time. At first he'll make a great to-do; by and by he too will find out it's better to live in the storeroom among the sides of bacon and sleep well at night than to catch a few mice one by one in the grain-loft. Go on! I know what regents are made of.

CARPENTER: What a fellow like that can get away with! If I'd ever said such a thing as that in my whole life I'd never feel safe for a second.

VANSEN: Don't you worry. God himself doesn't notice worms like you, to say nothing of the Regent!

JETTER: Slanderer!

VANSEN: I know of others who would be better off if, instead of being as brave as they are, they had some tailor's blood in their veins.

CARPENTER: What do you mean by that?

VANSEN: Hm! I mean the Count.

JETTER: Egmont! What has he to fear?

VANSEN: I'm a poor devil and I could live for a year on what he loses in an evening. Yet it might well be worth his while to give me his income for a whole year if in exchange he could have my head for a quarter of an hour.

JETTER: You think you're mighty clever. Why, the hairs on Egmont's head have more sense than your whole brain.

VANSEN: So you say! But not more subtlety. Gentlemen are always the first to deceive themselves. He ought not to be so trustful.

JETTER: What nonsense you talk! Such a great gentleman!

VANSEN: Exactly—because he's not a tailor.

JETTER: Hold your foul tongue!

VANSEN: I wish he had *your* kind of courage in his limbs for just one hour, to make him uneasy and nag and prick at him until he would leave the city.

JETTER: You're talking outright nonsense. He's as safe as the stars in the sky.

VANSEN: Did you ever see a star snuffed out? Presto—and it was gone.

JETTER: But who on earth will do anything to him?

VANSEN: Who? Will *you* do anything to stop it? Will *you* start a riot if they arrest him?

JETTER: Ah!

VANSEN: Would you risk your limbs for him?

SOEST: Eh!

VANSEN: (*mimicking them*) Ih! Oh! Uh! Wonder on right through the alphabet! That's how it is, and how it will be. God help him!

JETTER: What I wonder at is your brazen impudence. Such a noble, upright man should have anything to fear?

VANSEN: Wherever the scoundrel sits, he has the advantage. In the prisoner's dock he makes a fool of the judge. On the judge's bench he gleefully turns every accused man into a criminal. Why, I've had to copy out a document in which the court heaped praise and money on the commissioner for having cross-examined a poor honest devil they wanted to get hold of into a scoundrel.

CARPENTER: That's another bare-faced lie. What can they want to cross-examine out of a man when he's innocent?

VANSEN: You bird-brained fool, you! When there's nothing to be cross-examined *out*, they cross-examine it *in*! Honesty will make a man indiscreet and defiant too. First they question away quietly, and the prisoner is proud of his innocence, as it's called, and blurts out everything that a man who knew the ropes would keep dark. Then the examiner turns the man's answers into new questions and watches for even the smallest contradiction to appear; that's where he ties on his noose; and if the poor stupid devil lets himself be caught saying too much here or too little there, or takes it into his silly head to suppress some fact, or ever lets himself get frightened about some point—then we're on the right road! And, believe me, no beggarwoman pokes through a rubbish pile looking for rags more carefully than such a manufacturer of criminals finally succeeds, out of all these little, lop-sided, displaced, distorted, disjointed, inferred, admitted, denied indications and circumstances, in patching together at long last a straw-and-rag scarecrow, so that he can hang his victim in effigy at least. And the poor devil can thank God if he is still there to see himself hanged.

JETTER: His tongue hangs in the middle and wags both ways.

CARPENTER: All that may work well enough with flies. But wasps laugh at your spider-web.

VANSEN: It depends on what kind of spider spins it. Why, the lanky Duke has exactly the look of a garden-spider; not one of the fat-bellied kind, they're not so bad; but one of the long-legged, small-bodied variety that never gets fat no matter how much he eats and spins a very fine web but one that's all the tougher.

JETTER: Egmont is a Knight of the Golden Fleece; who would dare lay hands on him? He can only be tried by his peers, by the entire Order. It's your loose tongue and your bad conscience that make you talk such nonsense.

VANSEN: Do I think the less of him for it? It's all the same to me. He's an admirable gentleman. A couple of good friends of mine would have been hanged sure as fate in any other country, but he packed them off with a thrashing. Now get along with you! Go on! Even I advise you to now. I see another patrol coming this way; they don't look as if they were in any hurry to drink eternal brotherhood with us. We'll bide our time and just quietly see what happens. I have a couple of nieces and an uncle once or twice removed who owns a taproom; wait till these fellows have had a taste of *them*—if that won't tame them, they're out-and-out wolves.

SCENE TWO

The Palace of Culenberg, the DUKE OF ALBA'S *residence.* SILVA AND GOMEZ (*meeting*).

SILVA: Have you carried out the Duke's orders?

GOMEZ: To the letter. The regular patrols have all been instructed to arrive, at the time fixed, at various places that I have designated; meanwhile they will make the rounds of the city as usual, keeping order. No patrol knows what the others are to do; each thinks that the instructions affect only itself; and so the cordon can be drawn up in an instant, with all ways of access to the palace occupied. Do you know the Duke's reason for giving these orders?

SILVA: My way is to obey blindly. And whom is it easier to obey than the Duke?—for what happens very soon proves that what he ordered was right.

GOMEZ: Of course, of course. Nor does it surprise me that you are becoming as reserved and laconic as he is, since you have always to be with him. To me it seems strange, since I'm accustomed to the more easy-going Italian service. In loyalty and obedience I am the same as ever; but I've got into the habit of talking and arguing. Here you all hold your tongues and never let yourselves go for an instant. The Duke seems to me to be like a tower without a gateway, so that the garrison have to be men with wings. The other day at table when the talk fell on a man who is always cheerful and pleasant, I heard the Duke say he was like a low pothouse with a brandy sign hung out to attract idlers, beggars, and thieves.

SILVA: Didn't he get us here, for all his silence?

GOMEZ: There's no denying that. He certainly did! And anyone who saw the skill with which he brought the army here from Italy saw something worth seeing. Why, he practically wriggled his way past friend and enemy, French Royalists and French heretics, the Swiss and the Allies, maintained the strictest discipline, and accomplished, effortlessly and without a hitch, a march that was supposed to be so dangerous!—We have seen something and had a chance to learn something.

SILVA: Here too! Isn't everything as quiet and peaceful as if there had been no uprising?

GOMEZ: Well, everything was quiet enough even when we got here.

SILVA: Things have become very much quieter in the Provinces. If anyone makes a move now, it's to run away. But the Duke will soon have the roads closed to them too, I believe.

GOMEZ: This will put him in the King's good graces if nothing else ever did.

SILVA: And we cannot do better than to remain in his. When the King comes here, the Duke and anyone whom he recommends will certainly not go unrewarded.

GOMEZ: Do you think the King will come?

SILVA: So many preparations are being made that it seems highly probable.

GOMEZ: They do not convince me.

SILVA: Then keep your thoughts to yourself. For if the King does not intend to come, he certainly intends people to believe that he will.

(*Enter* FERDINAND, ALBA's *bastard son*)

FERDINAND: Hasn't my father come out yet?

SILVA: We are waiting for him.

FERDINAND: The Princes will soon be here.

GOMEZ: Are they to come today?

FERDINAND: Orange and Egmont.

GOMEZ: (*whispering to Silva*) I understand something.

SILVA: Then keep it to yourself.

(*Enter the* DUKE OF ALBA. *As he comes forward, the others step back.*)

ALBA: Gomez.

GOMEZ: (*coming forward*) My lord!

ALBA: You have distributed the guards and given them their orders?

GOMEZ: In every detail. The regular patrols—

ALBA: That will do. You will wait in the gallery. Silva will tell you at what moment you are to draw them in and occupy the ways of access to the palace. You know the rest.

GOMEZ: Yes, my Lord! (*Exit*)

ALBA: Silva!

SILVA: Here.

ALBA: All that I have long esteemed in you, courage, resolution, irresistible execution—show them this day.

SILVA: I thank you for the opportunity to show that I am what I have always been.

ALBA: The moment the Princes have been admitted to my presence, go instantly to arrest Egmont's private secretary. You have made all preparations to apprehend the others who have been designated?

SILVA: Trust to us. Their fate, like a correctly calculated eclipse, will overtake them punctually and terribly.

ALBA: Have you had them carefully watched?

SILVA: All of them, and Egmont most particularly. He is the only one who has not altered his behavior since you arrived. He spends the whole day first on one horse, then on another, entertains guests, is always gay and amusing at table, plays dice, shoots, and at night slips off to his sweetheart. The others, on the contrary, have obviously suspended all their normal activities; they stay at home alone, and their doorways look as if there were a sick man in the house.

ALBA: All the more reason for acting quickly, before they recover in spite of us!

SILVA: I'll bring them to bay! As you directed, we are treating them with the utmost respect and courtesy. It frightens them; they return us politic and nervous thanks, all the while feeling that the wisest thing to do would be to run away. None of them ventures on a step, they shilly-shally, cannot agree among themselves; at the same time loyalty to each other prevents any one of them from making a bold move alone. They would like nothing better than to avoid all suspicion, and constantly make themselves more suspect. I can see your whole plan successfully executed, and I rejoice.

ALBA: I rejoice only over things that have been accomplished—and not too readily over those; for something always remains to be considered and provided against. Fortune is capricious, she often honors what is trivial and worthless and discredits well-considered actions by a trivial outcome.—Wait until the Princes arrive, then give Gomez the order to occupy the streets and, for your part, make all speed to arrest Egmont's secretary and the others I have designated. As soon as that is done, return here to the palace and inform my son, so that he can bring me word while I am still conferring with the Princes.

SILVA: I hope that I may be worthy to appear before you this evening.

(ALBA *joins his son, who has been standing in the gallery.*)

SILVA: I dare not say it, but my hope is uncertain. I fear that things will not turn out as he intends. I see spirits before me; silent and thoughtful, they weigh the fates of princes and of many thousands. Slowly the pointer of their black scales swings back and forth; the judges appear to ponder deeply; finally one scale rises, the other sinks, breathed on by capricious fate, and the decision is made. (*Exit*)

ALBA: (*coming forward with* FERDINAND) How did you find the city?

FERDINAND: Everything seems set right again. As if merely for pastime, I rode up and down the streets. Your well distributed guards hold fear so tautly drawn that it dares not even whisper. The city looks like a field when the lightnings of a coming storm flash far away—not a bird, not a beast but is slinking hastily to cover.

ALBA: Did you see nothing else?

FERDINAND: Egmont with some of his people came riding into the marketplace. We greeted each other; his mount was an unbroken horse, which I could not help praising to him. "We must hasten to break horses," he called to me; "we shall soon be needing them." He said he would see me again later today, that he was coming to confer with you, at your request.

ALBA: He will see you again.

FERDINAND: Of all the knights I have met here, I like him best. It seems that we shall be friends.

ALBA: You still have your old fault of plunging in without due consideration. I recognize in you that recklessness of your mother's which threw her into my arms without a question or a condition. Appearances have persuaded you into making many dangerous connections too precipitately.

FERDINAND: Your will ever finds me docile.

ALBA: I forgive your young blood this rash friendliness, this unsuspecting good nature. Only do not forget what work I have been sent here to do, and what part in it I wish to give to you.

FERDINAND: Admonish me and do not spare me, wherever you consider it necessary.

ALBA: (after a moment) My son!

FERDINAND: My father!

ALBA: The Princes will soon be here; Orange and Egmont are coming. It is from no mistrust that I only now reveal to you what is to occur. They shall not leave this place.

FERDINAND: What are you planning?

ALBA: It has been decided to arrest them.—You are surprised! Listen, while I tell you what part you are to play; you shall learn the reasons after everything is accomplished. There is not time to explain them now. Only with you do

I wish to discuss the most important and most secret things; we are bound together by the strongest of ties; you are precious and dear to me; I would wish to give you all that I have. I would inculcate in you not only the habit of obedience, I would implant in you too the capacity to lay plans, to command, to execute; I would leave you the greatest of inheritances and the King his most useful servant; I would equip you with the best that I have, so that you need not feel ashamed to appear among your brothers.

FERDINAND: What do I not owe you for this love?—which you show to me alone, while a whole kingdom trembles before you.

ALBA: Hear now what is to be done. As soon as the Princes have arrived, every way of access to the palace will be occupied. Gomez has orders to attend to that. Silva will set off at once to arrest Egmont's secretary and the others who are most under suspicion. You will supervise the guards at the gate and in the courtyards. Above all, occupy the adjoining rooms with the most trustworthy men; then wait in the gallery until Silva returns, and, when he does, come in to me on the excuse of bringing me some paper or other, thus letting me know that Silva's mission is accomplished. Then wait in the anteroom until Orange leaves; follow him; I shall detain Egmont here, as if I had something more to say to him. When you reach the end of the gallery, demand Orange's sword and summon the guard; Orange is the most dangerous of all; secure him quickly, and I will seize Egmont here.

FERDINAND: I shall obey your commands, Father. For the first time with a heavy heart and anxious foreboding.

ALBA: I forgive you. It is the first great day in your experience.

(*Enter* SILVA)

SILVA: A messenger from Antwerp. Here is Orange's letter. He is not coming.

ALBA: Does the messenger say so?

SILVA: No. My heart tells me so.

ALBA: My evil genius speaks from you. (*He reads the letter, then signals to them and they withdraw to the gallery. He remains alone, stage front.*) He is not coming! He leaves it until the last moment to declare himself. He has the audacity not to come. So this time, contrary to all expectations, the clever man was clever enough not to be clever!—The clock moves on. The hand has but a little way to go, and a great work will be accomplished or fail, fail irreparably—for it can neither be retrieved nor kept secret. I had long considered everything maturely, thought even of this contingency, determined what should be done in this event too; and now that it is to be done, I can scarcely keep my mind from being unsettled once again by all the pros and cons.—Is it wise to seize the others when *he* escapes me?—Shall I put off acting, and let Egmont and his friends, his many friends, slip away, when at this moment, and perhaps today only, they are in my hands? Does fate, then, coerce even you, the indomitable? How long considered! How well prepared! How great, how beautifully contrived the plan! How near its goal the hope! And now, in the moment of decision, you find yourself between two evils; you reach into the dark future as into a lottery urn; the lot you draw is still folded, you know not what is contains, whether the prize or a blank! (*He listens, as if hearing something, and goes to the window.*) It is he!—Egmont! Did your horse bring you here so easily, and never shy at the smell of blood and the ghost with naked sword that stands at the gate to receive you?—Dismount!—Now you have one foot in the grave!—and now both!—Yes, stroke him and pat his neck for the last time for his spirited service—For me, no choice remains. Impossible that Egmont should deliver himself into your hands a second time under the delusion in which he comes here today!—You there! (FERDINAND *and* SILVA *hurry in.*) [*to* SILVA] Do what I ordered you. I shall not change my purpose. (*to* FERDINAND) I shall detain Egmont here on one pretext or another until you bring me word from Silva. Then remain within call. Fate robs you, too, of the noble service of arresting the King's greatest enemy with your own hand. (*to* SILVA) Be off! (*to* FERDINAND) Go to meet him! (ALBA *is left alone for a few moments, and paces back and forth in silence.*)

(*enter* EGMONT)

EGMONT: I have come to learn the King's commands, to hear what service he demands of our loyalty, which remains eternally his.

ALBA: Above all he wishes to receive your advice.

EGMONT: On what subject? Is Orange coming too? I thought he would be here.

ALBA: I regret to say that he has failed us at this critical hour. The King desires your advice, your opinion, as to how to restore these States to peace. He hopes, indeed, that you will cooperate energetically to quiet these disturbances and to lay a firm and enduring foundation for order in these Provinces.

EGMONT: You should know better than I that everything is reasonably peaceful already, and indeed was still more peaceful before the appearance of the new soldiers aroused fear and anxiety in the people's minds again.

ALBA: You seem to suggest that the wisest course would have been for the King not to have put me in a position to consult you.

EGMONT: Forgive me! Whether the King should have sent the army, whether the force of his own royal presence alone would not have produced a stronger effect, is not for me to judge. The army is here, and he is not. But we should have to be very ungrateful, very forgetful, if we did not remember what we owe to the Regent. Let us acknowledge it. Her no less wise than courageous behavior pacified the rioters, partly by force and authority, partly by persuasion and diplomacy, and, to the astonishment of the world, led a rebellious people back to its duty in a very few months.

ALBA: I do not deny it. The disorders are quelled, and all would seem to have been forced back within the bounds of obedience. But is it not a matter of individual whim whether those bounds are again overstepped? Who will keep the people from breaking loose? Where is the power to hold them back? Who vouches to us that they will continue to be loyal and submissive? Their good will is all the security we have.

EGMONT: And is the good will of a people not the strongest and the noblest security? By God! when can a king feel himself more secure than when all stand for one and one for all? More secure against both domestic and foreign enemies?

ALBA: You can hardly expect us to persuade ourselves that such is the case here at this moment?

EGMONT: Let the King issue a general pardon, let him thus tranquilize the people's minds; and it will soon be evident how loyalty and love return with trust and confidence.

ALBA: And everyone who insulted the King's majesty and the sanctity of religion would be turned loose to go wherever he pleased, to bear living witness that atrocious crimes bring no punishment?

EGMONT: And should not a crime committed in frenzy, in intoxication, rather be forgiven than cruelly punished? Especially when there is assured hope, when there is certainty that the evil will not recur? Have not kings thus been more secure? Are they not praised by the world and posterity, who could forgive, pity, disregard an offense against their dignity? Are they not for that very reason likened to God, who is far too great for every little blasphemy to reach him?

ALBA: And that precisely is why the King must champion the dignity of God and religion, and why we must fight for the King's authority. What one above us disdains to resent, it is our duty to avenge. So long as my voice is heeded, no guilty person shall congratulate himself on getting off unpunished.

EGMONT: Do you believe that you will reach them *all?* Do we not hear every day that fear is driving them hither and yon, out of the country? The richest will flee with their possessions, their children, and their friends; the poor man will bring his useful hands to a neighboring country.

ALBA: They will if we do not find means to stop them. That is why the King demands counsel and action from every Prince, earnest endeavor from every Stadholder— not mere accounts of how matters stand and what might result if everything is allowed to go on just as it is going. To witness a great evil, and flatter oneself with hope, to trust to time, and perhaps strike out, as in a carnival play, just in order to make a noise and seem to be doing something when one would like to do nothing—is not this to invite being suspected of looking on with satisfaction at an uprising that one would not incite but is more than willing to nurture?

EGMONT: (*about to break out, controls himself and after a moment's silence speaks calmly*) Not every intention is obvious, and many men's intentions are open to misinterpretation. Even the King's. One cannot but hear, from every direction, that his intention is less to govern the Provinces

by uniform and unequivocal laws, to safeguard the majesty
of religion, and to give his people a general peace, than to
put them unconditionally under the yoke, to rob them of
their ancient rights, to make himself master of their possessions, to curtail the admirable rights of the nobility
which alone make it possible for any man of gentle blood
to serve him even to the sacrifice of life and limb. Religion,
it is rumored, is merely a magnificent tapestry, behind
which it is all the easier to plan the most dangerous strokes.
The people crouch on their knees praying to the embroidered symbols of sanctity, and the birdcatcher lurks
behind, waiting for his chance to ensnare them.

ALBA: Must I hear this from *you?*

EGMONT: These are not *my* thoughts. They are only
what is being rumored everywhere, by great and small
alike, by intelligent men and fools. The Netherlanders fear
a twofold yoke—and who stands security to them for their
freedom?

ALBA: Freedom! A fine word, if it were rightly understood!
What freedom do they want? What is the freedom of the
freest?—To do right!—And the King will not prevent them
from doing that. No, no, they think they are not free because they cannot do harm to themselves and others.
Would it not be better to abdicate than to rule such a
people? When external enemies threaten, the citizens are
so occupied with their own concerns that they do not even
know it until the King demands their aid—and then all
they do is to bicker among themselves, which amounts to

conspiring with their enemies. Far better to hold them within strict limits, so that they can be controlled like children, guided for their good, like children. Believe me, a people never grows up, never reaches the age of discretion; a people is always a child.

EGMONT: How seldom does a King achieve understanding! And shall not many trust many far rather than one?—and not even the one, but the few around him, the tribe who grow up under the eyes of their lord and master! They alone, it appears, have the right to attain discretion.

ALBA: Perhaps precisely because they are not left to their own devices.

EGMONT: And hence are unwilling to see anyone else left to his. Let what action has been decided on be taken—I have answered your question, and I repeat: it won't do, it will never do! I know my fellow countrymen. They are men fit to walk God's earth—every man of them complete in himself, a little king, steadfast, active, capable, loyal, staunchly attached to tradition. It is hard to deserve their trust, but easy to keep it once it is earned. Stubborn and steadfast! They can be pressed, but not oppressed.

ALBA: (*who has looked around several times during Egmont's speech*) Would you repeat all this in the King's presence?

EGMONT: So much the worse, if his presence should intimidate me. So much the better for him, for his people, if he gave me courage, inspired me with confidence to say far more than I have said.

ALBA: Anything worth hearing, I can hear as well as he.

EGMONT: I would say to him: The shepherd can easily drive a whole flock of sheep before him; the ox draws his plough unresistingly; but if you would ride a noble horse, you must learn how he thinks, you must not ask him to do anything unreasonable or unreasonably. The citizen wants to keep his ancient constitution, to be governed by his fellow countrymen, because he knows how he will be handled, because he can expect disinterestedness from them and sympathy in his lot.

ALBA: And is the King's Regent to have no power to change these old traditions? Should not precisely that be his most noble privilege? What is enduring in this world? And is a particular form of government alone to escape change? Must not every relation alter in the course of time and an ancient constitution become the cause of a thousand evils for the very reason that it does not embrace the present situation of the people? I am very much afraid that these ancient rights are so highly esteemed because they provide loopholes for the crafty and the powerful to hide in or escape through, to the detriment of the people, of the whole body politic.

EGMONT: And these arbitrary changes, these unrestrained interventions of the highest power—do they not proclaim that one man has determined to do what thousands are not to do? He intends to allow himself alone freedom, so that he can satisfy his every wish, execute his every thought. And suppose that, as a good and wise king, we should trust him entirely—can he be answerable to us for his successors? can he assure us that not one of them will ever rule mercilessly, ruthlessly? Then who is to protect us against the most arbitrary caprice if he sends us his servants, his favorites, men who, having no knowledge of the country or its needs, govern as they please, meet no resistance, and know that they are responsible to no one?

ALBA: (*who has meanwhile been looking about again*) Nothing is more natural than that a king should expect to rule in his own person and should choose to have his commands carried out by those who best understand him and seek to understand him and who execute his will unconditionally.

EGMONT: And it is just as natural that the citizen should wish to be ruled by one born and brought up with him, who has arrived at the same conception of right and wrong as himself, and whom he can regard as his brother.

ALBA: Yet the nobility have shared very unequally with these brothers of theirs.

EGMONT: That came about centuries ago, and is now accepted without grudging. But if new men, sent when there is no need for them, should a second time seek to enrich themselves at the expense of the nation, if the people found themselves exposed to exacting, uncontrolled, and unashamed avarice—that would raise a tumult which would not easily subside of itself.

ALBA: You say to me what I should not hear; I too am a foreigner in this country.

EGMONT: That I say it to you proves that I do not mean you.

ALBA: Even so, I prefer not to hear it from you. The King sent me here in the hope that I should find support from the nobility. The King wills what he wills. After profound deliberation, the King has seen what is good for the people; things cannot continue as they have been going. The King's purpose is to lay restrictions on the people for their own good; if need be, to force their own welfare on them; to sacrifice the pernicious so that the rest of the citizens can be at peace, can enjoy the happiness of living under a wise government. That is his decision; and I have been ordered to announce it to the nobility. And the advice that I demand in his name is how best to put it into effect, not what to put into effect, for *he* has determined that.

EGMONT: Alas, your words justify the fears of the people, the fear that is everywhere! So he has determined what no prince should determine. The strength of his people, their spirit, their very conception of themselves, is to be undermined, repressed, destroyed, so that he may rule them easily. He means to pervert their inmost being—of course, in order to make them happier. He means to annihilate them so that they may become something, something other than what they are. Oh, if his intentions are good, they are misguided! It is not the royal power that is resisted; the resistance is only against the king who is taking the first unhappy step along the wrong path.

ALBA: Since these are your views, it would appear to

be useless for us to try to agree. You think too little of the King and too contemptuously of his councillors if you suppose that everything you have said has not already been considered and tested and weighed. I have no commission to go through every argument on either side all over again. What I demand of the people is obedience; and of you to whom they look up as their exemplars, who are their feudal lords, I demand advice and action, I demand that you make yourselves responsible for the performance of this unconditional duty.

EGMONT: Demand our heads, and have it over with at once. Whether his neck bows under such a yoke, whether he crouches down before the block, is all one to a man of noble soul. In vain have I spoken at such length; I have stirred the air and done no more.

(*Enter* FERDINAND)

FERDINAND: Excuse my interrupting your conversation. Here is a letter whose bearer is such that an immediate answer seems imperative.

ALBA: If you will allow me, I will see what it contains. (*He goes aside.*)

FERDINAND: (*to* EGMONT) That's a fine horse your people have brought for you to ride home.

EGMONT: I've seen worse. I have had it for some time; I've been thinking of getting rid of it. If you like it, we can probably come to terms.

FERDINAND: Good. We'll see.

(ALBA *motions to his son, who retires stage rear.*)

EGMONT: Good-bye! Permit me to take my leave. For, by God, I do not know what more to say.

ALBA: Chance has fortunately prevented you from speaking your mind further. You incautiously lay bare your own heart, and yourself accuse yourself more rigorously than any enemy could do out of hatred for you.

EGMONT: Your reproach does not touch me. I know myself well enough, and know how devoted I am to the King —far more than many who, in his service, serve themselves. It is most unwillingly that I abandon this discussion without seeing our differences reconciled; and I only hope that our Master's service and the good of the country may soon unite us. Perhaps another conversation, the presence of the other Princes who are absent today will, at a more propitious time, accomplish what today seems impossible. With this hope I leave you.

ALBA: (simultaneously signaling to his son FERDINAND) Stop, Egmont!—Your sword!—
(The center door opens, the gallery is visible, occupied by motionless guards.)

EGMONT: (after a moment of astonished silence) Was this your purpose? Was it for this that you summoned me? (Reaching for his sword, as if to defend himself) But I am not unarmed!

ALBA: By the King's command, you are my prisoner.
(As he speaks, armed men enter from either side.)

EGMONT: (after a silence) The King?—Orange! Orange! (He pauses for a moment, then surrenders his sword.)

Take it! It has far oftener supported the King's cause than defended this breast.

(*Exit* EGMONT *through the center door, the armed men who have entered the room following him, then* ALBA'S *son.* ALBA *stands motionless. The curtain falls.*)

ACT V

A Street. Twilight. CLARA. BRACKENBURG. *Citizens.*

BRACKENBURG: Dearest, for Heaven's sake, what do you mean to do?

CLARA: Come with me, Brackenburg. It must be that you do not know these men.—We shall free him, never fear! For what is as great as their love of him? I would swear that every one of them is on fire to save him, to avert this danger to a precious life, and restore the freest of men to freedom. Come! All that is wanted is the voice to summon them together. What they owe him is still fresh and living in their minds; and they know that only his strong arm holds off their destruction. For his sake and their own they cannot but risk all. And what do we risk? At most our lives, which are not worth keeping if he perishes.

BRACKENBURG: Unhappy Clara! You do not see what power holds us in fetters of iron.

CLARA: I see it, and I think it is not insurmountable. Let us not waste time in useless argument. Here come some of the old honest, brave men! A word with you, friends! Neighbors, a word!—What news of Egmont?

93

CARPENTER: What does the girl want? Make her hold her tongue!

CLARA: Come closer, so that we may speak softly, until we are united and stronger. We must not lose a minute! The overweening tyranny that dares to imprison him is drawing the dagger to murder him. O friends, with every darkening moment of twilight I grow more anxious. I fear this night. Come! Let us divide into groups and run from street to street, calling out the citizens. Let each man snatch up his old weapon. We will meet again in the market-place, the flood of us will carry everyone along. The enemy will find themselves surrounded, engulfed, smothered. What sort of resistance can a handful of hirelings oppose to us? And *he* will return among us, freed, and for once *he* can be grateful to *us*, who are so deeply in his debt. Perhaps he will—no—he *will* see the dawn in freedom, under the open sky.

CARPENTER: What ails you, girl?

CLARA: Can you misunderstand me? I mean the Count! Egmont!

CARPENTER: Do not speak that name. It is deadly.

CLARA: Not that name? What! Not his name? Who does not speak it in season and out of season? Where is it not written? In these very stars I have often read it, letter by letter! Not name it? What do you mean? Friends! Dear, faithful neighbors, you are dreaming; gather your wits together. Do not stare at me with such fear in your eyes.

Stop looking about you so timidly. What I am saying to you is only what everyone desires. Is not my voice the voice of your own hearts? Who among you in this anxious night would not, before he seeks his restless bed, go down on his knees to win him from Heaven by most earnest prayer? Ask one another! each of you ask himself! and who among you will not say with me: "Egmont freed, or death!"

JETTER: Heaven protect us! This will end badly.

CLARA: Stay! Stay! Crowd not away now from his name, around which once you pressed so joyously!—When rumor announced his arrival, when you heard, "Egmont is coming! He is on his way from Ghent!" those who lived in the streets through which he would ride thought themselves in luck. And when you heard the hooves of his horses, each of you dropped his work, and over all the anxious-looking faces that you thrust out of windows a look of joy and hope passed like a sunbeam at sight of him. You held up your children in your doorways and pointed to him, saying, "Look, that's Egmont, the tallest man there! It is he! It is he from whom you may yet one day hope for better times than your poor parents have known." Let not your children one day ask of you: "Where has he gone? Where are the better times that you once promised us?"—And we stand here talking, do nothing, betray him.

SOEST: Shame on you, Brackenburg. Don't let her go on. Stop her before there's trouble.

BRACKENBURG: Dear Clara, let us go! What will your mother say? Perhaps—

CLARA: Do you think me a child, or mad? What good is "perhaps"? You cannot lure me from this terrible certainty by hopes.—Friends, you must hear me, and you shall; for I see that you are dismayed and cannot find yourselves in your own hearts. Through present danger cast but a single glance into the past, the most recent past. Turn your thoughts to the future. Could you live, would you be alive, if he perishes? When he breathes no more, the last breath of freedom is fled. What was he to you? For whom did he freely risk the gravest danger? His wounds bled and healed for you alone. The great soul that upbore you all is confined to a dungeon, haunted by all the horrors of treachery and murder. Perhaps he thinks of you, perhaps he hopes in you—he whose part it has ever been to give, to fulfill.

CARPENTER: Come, neighbor.

CLARA: I have neither your arms nor your stamina; but I have that which none of you has, courage and scorn of danger. O that my breath could kindle you! O that I could clasp you to my bosom, and so heat and animate you! Come! I will go with you! As a flag, waving unarmed, leads on a noble host of warriors, so shall my spirit flame about your heads, and love and courage shall unite the doubtful, divided people into a terrible host.

JETTER: Take her away; I feel sorry for her.

(*Exeunt Citizens*)

BRACKENBURG: Clara! Do you not see where we are?

CLARA: Where? Under the sky, that often seemed all the more magnificent when his nobility walked free beneath it.

It was from these same windows that they looked out, four or five heads at each, one above the other. It was in front of these same doors that they scraped and bowed when he looked down at them, the cowards! O, I loved them so well, when they honored him! If he had been a tyrant, they would be right to scatter from his fall. But they loved him! —O you hands, so ready to bare your heads, can you not bare your swords—And we, Brackenburg? Do *we* reproach them? These arms that so often embraced him—what are they doing for him?—Ruse has accomplished so many things in this world—You know your way about, you know the old castle. Nothing is impossible, give me some plan!

BRACKENBURG: Let us go home!

CLARA: Very well.

BRACKENBURG: There at the corner I see Alba's guard. Let the voice of reason find your heart. Do you think me a coward? Do you not believe that I would die for your sake? Here we are both mad, I as mad as you. Do you not see how impossible it is? Regain your self-possession! You are beside yourself.

CLARA: Beside myself! Monstrous! Brackenburg, it is you who are beside yourself! When you spoke out in praise of the hero, when you called him friend and protector and hope of the country, when you cheered him at his coming —I stood there in my corner, half opened the window, hid myself to look on, and my heart beat higher than the heart of any man among you. Now, again, it beats higher than the heart of any man among you! Now that there is danger, you hide, you deny him, and you do not understand that you are doomed if he perishes.

BRACKENBURG: Come home.

CLARA: Home?

BRACKENBURG: Come to your senses. Look around you. These are the streets where you never set foot except on Sundays, when you went modestly to church, the streets where your exaggerated sense of propriety took offence if I approached you with a friendly greeting. You stand here talking and acting before the eyes of the whole world. Come to your senses, dearest. What good can this do us?

CLARA: Home, then! Yes, I have come to my senses. Come Brackenburg, I will go home! Do you know where my home is?

(*Exeunt*)

SCENE TWO

A dungeon, lighted by a lamp, a cot at stage rear.

EGMONT: (*alone*) Old friend, ever faithful sleep, do you too flee me, like my other friends? How willingly you sank upon my head when it was free, cooling my temples like the fairest myrtle wreath of love! In a world of weapons, on the heaving swell of life, I rested in your arms, breathing as lightly as a growing boy. When storms roared through twigs and leaves, and the whole tree, branch and crown, swayed and creaked, the inmost core of my heart remained unmoved. What shakes it now? What shakes my firm, steadfast mind? I feel it, it is the ringing stroke of the death-axe, gnawing into my root. Though still I stand upright, I shudder inwardly. Yes, the treacherous power prevails; it undermines the tall firm trunk, and before the bark dries up, the crown comes crashing down and shatters to fragments.

Why, when you have so often brushed immense cares from your mind like soap-bubbles, can you not dispel this premonition that now haunts you in a thousand guises? Since when has death seemed terrifying to you? Have you not lived with its changing shapes as calmly as with the other figures of this familiar earth? But it is not the swift enemy, the death to which the healthy spirit hastens in emulous rivalry; it is the dungeon, image of the grave, no less abhorrent to the hero than to the coward. Already I found it intolerable to remain sitting in my cushioned chair when the Princes assembled in council would make speech after speech over something that could easily have been decided without discussion, and the dark walls and the beamed ceiling of the state chamber stifled me. As soon as I could I would hurry out, and drawing a deep breath, mount my horse. And then away! out where we belong, into the open fields, where the earth exhales every immediate benison of nature and all the favorable influences of the planets breathe on us from the sky; where, like the earth-born giant, we spring up again the stronger from touching our mother; where we feel our whole humanity,

our whole human striving in every vein; where the urge
to press on, to conquer, to gain, to use his fist, to possess,
to triumph burns in the young hunter's soul; where the
soldier, in swift march, makes good his native right to the
whole world, and, like a hailstorm over meadow, field, and
forest, moves on destroying, knowing no boundaries set
by human hands.

You are but an image now, remembered dream of the
happiness that was mine for so long; and where has
treacherous Fate borne you away? Does she refuse to grant
you the death you never feared, swift death in the light
of the sun, only to give you a foretaste of the grave in
nauseous damps? How loathesomely it breathes upon me
from these stones! Life stiffens already, and my foot shrinks
from that cot as from the grave.—

O care, care, which begins the assassin's work before
its time, desist!—Since when is Egmont alone, so wholly
alone in this world? It is doubt that makes you helpless, it
is not fate. Has the justice of the King, in which you have
trusted all your life, has the Regent's friendship, which was
almost—you may admit it—almost love: have they both
vanished all at once, like a fiery meteor of night, leaving
you behind, alone on a dark path? Will not Orange, at the
head of your friends, plan boldly? Will not the people
come together, and with gathering power rescue their old
friend?

O walls that shut me in, keep not the friendly zeal of so
many hearts from me; and whatever courage once flooded

and filled them from my eyes, may it now return from their
hearts to mine! Yes, yes! they are rising in their thousands!
They are coming! They are with me! Their urgent prayer
rises to heaven, imploring a miracle. And if an angel come
not down to save me, I see them seizing sword and lance.
The gates burst, the bars yield, the walls fall under their
hands, and Egmont rises to meet the freedom of the dawn-
ing day in joy. How many familiar faces receive me with
jubilation! Ah, Clara, if you were a man, I should see you
here first of them all, and owe you what it is hard to owe
even to a king—freedom!

SCENE THREE

CLARA's *House.* CLARA *enters from her room with a lamp
and a glass of water; she sets the glass on the table and
goes to the window.*

CLARA: Brackenburg? Is it you? Then what did I hear?
Still no one? It was no one! I will put the lamp in the
window, so that he will see that I am still watching, still
waiting for him. He promised me news. News? Horrible
certainty!—Egmont sentenced!—What court dare even
summon him? And they sentence him? The King condemns
him? Or it is the Duke? And the Regent stands aside!
Orange hesitates, and all his friends!——Is this the world,
of whose fickleness and untrustworthiness I have heard so
much and experienced nothing? Is this the world?—Who

could be wicked enough to hate him who is so dearly loved? Could wickedness be strong enough to overthrow him whose merits are declared by all? Yet it is true—it is true! O Egmont, I believe you safe before God and men, safe as in my arms! What was I to you? You called me yours, I consecrated my whole life to your life.—What am I *now*? Vainly I stretch out my hand to the noose that threatens you. You helpless, and I free!—Here is the key to my house door. I can come and go as I will, and I am of no use to you!——O fetter me, that I may not despair, cast me into the deepest dungeon, that I may beat my head against oozing walls, whimper for freedom, dream how I would long to help him if fetters did not cripple me, how I *would* help him.—Now I am free! And in freedom lies the agony of impotence.—In full control of my senses, yet unable to move a limb to help him. Alas, even that small part of your being, your Clara, is fettered too, and, parted from you, only expends her last strength in the convulsions of death.—I hear soft footsteps, a cough—Brackenburg—it is he!—Kind, unhappy man, your fate is ever the same; the girl you love opens the door to you at night, and ah! to what an unhappy meeting!

(*Enter* BRACKENBURG)

CLARA: You look so pale and frightened, Brackenburg! What is it?

BRACKENBURG: I could not come here directly, it is too dangerous. The main streets are occupied; I came slinking through lanes and alleys.

CLARA: Speak. What is happening?

BRACKENBURG: (*sitting down*) Ah, Clara, let me weep. I did not love him. He was the rich man and he lured the poor man's one ewe lamb to better pastures. I never cursed him; God made me loyal and soft-natured. My life flowed out of me in grief, and every day I hoped would see me pine away.

CLARA: Forget that, Brackenburg. Forget yourself. Tell me of him! Is it true? Is he condemned?

BRACKENBURG: He is. I know it for a certainty.

CLARA: But he is still alive?

BRACKENBURG: Yes, he is still alive.

CLARA: How can you be sure of that? Tyranny murders the hero in the dark of night! His blood flows hidden from every eye. The stunned people lie in ominous sleep and dream of saving him, dream the fulfillment of their impotent wish; meanwhile, despising us, his great soul leaves the world. He is dead!—Do not deceive me, do not deceive yourself!

BRACKENBURG: No, he is alive!—And the Spaniard, alas! is setting the stage for a terrible spectacle for the people whom he is determined to crush, a spectacle such that the sheer force of it will forever fill with despair every heart that still beats for freedom.

CLARA: Go on, and calmly pronounce my death sentence too. I walk closer and closer to the fields of the blessed, already comfort is wafted to me from those abodes of peace. Speak on.

BRACKENBURG: From a word here, a word there dropped
by the guards, I made out that something horrible was being
secretly prepared in the market-place. Taking byways and
familiar alleys, I stole to my cousin's house; there, from a
back window, I looked out into the market-place.—Torches
swayed back and forth, around a great circle of Spanish
soldiers. I strained my unaccustomed eyes, and a wide,
high scaffold loomed black against the darkness; the sight
of it made me shudder. A number of men were busy about
it, draping black cloth over what wood yet remained white
and uncovered. Finally they draped the steps in black too
—I saw it clearly. They seemed to be preparing to con-
summate some terrible sacrifice. Some of them now set
up a tall white crucifix to one side; in the darkness it
gleamed like silver. As I watched, I saw the terrible certainty ever more clearly. For a time torches still moved here
and there; little by little they grew dimmer and went out.
And suddenly the monstrous offspring of the darkness returned to the womb that had given it birth.

CLARA: Silence, Brackenburg! Be still! Let that veil rest
upon my soul. The specters have vanished; and do thou,
pure night, lend thy mantle to the laboring earth! no longer
will she endure the monstrous burden; shuddering, she
opens her abysses and swallows the murderous scaffold. And
the God whom they have reviled by making him the witness of their wrath sends down an angel; at his touch,
locks and fetters open, the blessed messenger sheds a gentle
light about our friend, and silently, gently, leads him forth

to freedom. And my way too leads through this shrouding darkness, to meet him.

BRACKENBURG: (*stopping her*) Child, where are you going? What project dare you entertain?

CLARA: Hush, dear. Let us not waken anyone! not even ourselves! Do you recognize this vial, Brackenburg. I took it from you in play when you used impatiently to threaten that you would hasten your own end.—And now, my friend—

BRACKENBURG: In the name of all the saints!—

CLARA: You cannot stop me. Death is my portion! grant me the swift, the gentle death that you had prepared for yourself. Give me your hand!—At this moment, when I open the dark door from which there is no return, would that with this pressure of my hand I could tell you how much I have loved you, how much I have pitied you. My brother died young; I chose you to take his place. Your heart gainsaid it and tortured itself and me; more and more passionately you demanded what was not destined for you. Forgive me, and farewell! Let me call you brother. It is a name that contains many names. With loyal heart, receive this last fair flower from one departing—receive this kiss— Death unites all things, Brackenburg. So it unites us too.

BRACKENBURG: Then let me die with you! Share with me, share! There is enough of it to quench two lives.

CLARA: Stay! you must live, you can live.—Help my mother, without you she would waste away in poverty. Be to her what I can be no longer. Remain together and mourn for me. Mourn for our country, and for him who alone could have maintained it. They who are alive this day will never be freed from this grief; not even the fury of vengeance will suffice to dispel it. Live on, wretches, live out the age that is no more an age. Today the world stands suddenly still; its circulation ceases, and my pulse beats on but a few moments more. Farewell!

BRACKENBURG: O, live with us, as we live for you alone! You kill us in yourself, O, live and endure. We will stand by you at either side and never leave you, and ever shall love hold forth its living arms to you, offering its most precious consolation. Be ours! Ours! I dare not say "mine."

CLARA: Softly, Brackenburg. You know not what you touch. Where you feel hope, I know despair.

BRACKENBURG: Share hope with the living! Pause on the edge of the abyss, gaze down into it, and look back at us.

CLARA: I have conquered. Summon me not back to strife.

BRACKENBURG: You are bewildered; wrapped in darkness, you seek the depths. All light is not extinguished yet; day will come, and many days.

CLARA: Woe! Woe upon you, and again woe! Cruelly have you torn the curtain from before my eyes. Yes, it will dawn! In vain will this fatal day draw every cloud about it and dawn unwillingly! The citizen looks from his window with terror, night has left a black stain; he looks, and the murderous scaffold looms fearfully in the light. Its agony renewed, the desecrated holy image raises imploring eyes to the Father. The sun does not venture forth! it refuses to mark the hour in which *he* must die. Slowly the clock-hands follow their course, and hour after hour strikes. Stop! Stop! now is the hour come! Fear of the morning drives me to the grave. (*She goes to the window, as if to look out, and secretly drinks.*)

BRACKENBURG: Clara! Clara!

CLARA: (*goes to the table and drinks the glass of water*) Here is what is left! I do not ask you to follow me. Do what you think right—farewell. Put out the lamp quietly and at once; I go to rest. Steal softly away and shut the door behind you. Be silent. Do not wake my mother. Go, save yourself! Save yourself, if you would not appear to have been my murderer. (*Exit*)

BRACKENBURG: She leaves me this last time, as she has always left me. O, were there a soul on earth that could feel how she can tear a loving heart. She leaves me standing here, abandons me to myself; and death and life are alike loathsome to me.—To die alone! Weep, ye lovers! There is no harder fate than mine! She shares the mortal drops with me, and sends me away! away from her side! She draws me after her, and thrusts me back into life. O Egmont, how cheaply bought the lot that falls to you! She goes before you; the victor's crown is yours from her hand; with her, all Heaven comes to meet you!—And shall I follow? once again stand aside? carry my inextinguishable envy into those abodes?—No more can I remain on earth, and Hell and Heaven offer the same torments. Ah, the dread hand of utter annihilation—how welcome were it to my misery!

(*Exit. For a few moments the stage remains unchanged. Then music, signifying Clara's death, begins. The lamp, which Brackenburg had forgotten to extinguish, flares up once or twice, then goes out.*)

SCENE FOUR

The Dungeon. EGMONT *lies asleep on the cot. There is a rattling of keys, and the door opens. Servants with torches enter; they are followed by* FERDINAND, ALBA'S *son, and* SILVA, *accompanied by armed men.* EGMONT *starts out of his sleep.*)

EGMONT: Who are you that thus rudely shake sleep from my eyes? What do your defiant and uneasy looks foretell for me? What means this dread train? What lying nightmare do you bring to my half-awakened mind?

SILVA: The Duke sends us to announce your sentence to you.

EGMONT: And have you brought the headsman with you to execute it?

SILVA: Hear it, and you will know what awaits you.

EGMONT: This is in perfect keeping with yourselves and with your infamous undertaking. In darkness hatched, in darkness carried out. Thus can this insolent act of injustice conceal itself!—Step boldly forth, he among you who hides the sword under his cloak; here is my head, the freest head that ever tyranny has parted from its body.

SILVA: You are wrong. What just judges decide, they will not hide from the face of day.

EGMONT: Then insolence exceeds all thought and imagination.

SILVA: (*takes the sentence from an attendant standing near him, unfolds it, and reads*) "In the King's name and by virtue of special powers transferred to us by His Majesty, to judge all his subjects of whatever rank, including Knights of the Golden Fleece, we declare—"

EGMONT: Can the King transfer those powers?

SILVA: "—we declare, after a previous thorough and legal investigation, that you, Henry Count Egmont, Prince of Gavre, are guilty of high treason and we pronounce sentence: that at earliest dawn you shall be conducted from prison to the market-place and there in the presence of all the people and as a warning to all traitors shall be sent from life to death by the sword. Given at Brussels this" (*The day of the month and the year are read indistinctly so that they are not perceptible to the audience.*)

"Ferdinand, Duke of Alba,
President of the Council of Twelve."

You now know your fate; but little time is left you to resign yourself to it, to set your affairs in order, and take leave of your kindred and friends.

(*Exit* SILVA *with his attendants.* FERDINAND *remains behind*

with two torches; the stage is dimly illuminated. EGMONT
has stood motionless and sunk in thought for a time, with-
out glancing around, and has let SILVA *go without looking*
up. He thinks that he is alone, but when he raises his eyes,
he sees ALBA'S *son.)*

EGMONT: You stand there? You remain? Do you seek
to increase my amazement, my horror by your presence?
Or perhaps you hope to carry your father the welcome mes-
sage that I gave way to cowardly despair? Go! Tell him,
tell him that he deceives neither me nor the world. He
will be known for what he is, he and his craving for fame!
First, it will be whispered behind his back, then spoken
louder and louder, and when one day he shall descend from
this peak of power, a thousand voices will shout it into his
ears: It was not the welfare of the state, not the honor of
the King, not the peace of the Provinces that brought him
here. It was for his own sake that he counseled war, so that
in war the soldier could shine. He instigated this monstrous
disturbance, so that he should be needed. And I fall, a
sacrifice to his base hate, his mean envy. Yes, I know it
and I dare to say it—the dying man, carrying his death-
wound, dares to speak it out: in his conceit he envied me,
and he has long sought and pondered how to extirpate me.

Even in those early days when we played dice together,
and one after another the piles of coins sped from his side
to mine, he stood there fuming, pretended to be calm, but
inwardly he was devoured by chagrin, more at my good luck
than at his losses. I still remember his blazing eyes, his be-

traying pallor when, at a public festival, we shot in competition before many thousands. He challenged me, and the two nations stood by; Spaniards and Netherlanders made their wagers and hoped. I was victorious over him; his ball missed, mine found the mark; a great cheer from my countrymen rent the air. This time his shot finds me. Tell him that I know it, that I know him, that the world despises every trophy of victory that a small man finds underhanded means to erect to himself. As for you—if it is possible for a son to turn from his father's ways, learn shame before it is too late, by being ashamed of him whom you would fain honor with all your heart.

FERDINAND: I have heard you out without interrupting you. Your reproaches fall as heavily as bludgeon blows on a helmet; I feel the shock, but I am armed. You strike me, you do not wound me; all that I feel is the grief that rends my breast. Alas for me! Alas! That I should have lived to witness such a sight! That I should have been sent to behold such a spectacle!

EGMONT: You give way to lamentations? What moves you, what troubles you? Is it belated remorse at having lent your aid to this infamous conspiracy? You are so young, your looks bode no evil. You were so friendly and confiding toward me. So long as you were in my sight, I felt reconciled to your father. Yet you are as much a dissembler as he, and more—for it was you who lured me into the trap. It is you who are the monster! Who trusts *him*, does it at his peril; but who would see peril in trusting you? Go, go!

Rob me not of these few minutes. Go, that I may collect myself, forget the world, and first of all you!—

FERDINAND: What can I say to you? I stand and look at you, and I do not see you and do not feel myself. Shall I exculpate myself? Shall I assure you that my father's purposes were not revealed to me until late, until the very last, that what I did I did as an unwitting, inanimate tool of his will? What does it matter what you may think me? You are lost; and I, wretch, but stand here to assure you of it, to mourn your fate.

EGMONT: What strange tones, what unexpected comfort do I find on my road to the grave? You, son of my first and almost my only enemy—you pity me, you are not one of my assassins? Speak, speak! Whom am I to see in you?

FERDINAND: Cruel father! Yes, I recognize you in this mission. You knew my heart, my nature, which you so often censured as the legacy of a too tender mother. It was to make me like yourself that you sent me here. You force me to look upon this man on the brink of the yawning grave, delivered over to a tyrannous death, so that I shall experience the deepest pain, become insensible to any fate, feel nothing, no matter what befalls me.

EGMONT: I am astounded. Control yourself. Stand up and speak like a man.

FERDINAND: Would that I were a woman! Would that I could decently be asked: What moves you, what is agitating you? Tell me of a greater, more monstrous evil, show me a more horrible deed—I will thank you, I will say that it was nothing.

EGMONT: You are losing control of youself! Do you know where you are?

FERDINAND: Let my passion rage, let me lament unrestrained. I will not appear to be firm when within me everything is shattered. Must I see you *here?* You?—it is horrible. You do not understand me! How should you understand me? Egmont! Egmont! (*Falling on his neck*)

EGMONT: Reveal this mystery.

FERDINAND: There is no mystery.

EGMONT: Why does the fate of a stranger move you so deeply?

FERDINAND: No stranger! You are no stranger to me! From my earliest boyhood your name shone for me like a star in the heavens. How often have I listened for news of you, asked for news of you! The child's hope is the youth, the youth's hope is the man. So you strode on before me; ever ahead, and without envy I saw you ahead and followed in your footsteps, on and on. Then at last I hoped to see you, and I saw you and my heart flew out to you. I had chosen you, and I chose you anew when I saw you. Then at last I hoped to be with you, to live with you, to know you, to—now all that is cast away, and I see you here!

EGMONT: My friend, if it can mean anything to you, know that I was drawn to you from the first moment. Now listen to me. Let us speak quietly together. Tell me—is it your father's settled and serious purpose to kill me?

FERDINAND: It is.

EGMONT: This death-sentence was not an empty scare-crow, to frighten me, to punish me by terror and threats, to abase me and then with royal condescension to raise me up again?

FERDINAND: No, alas! no. At first I flattered myself with the same devious hope; and even then it frightened and grieved me to see you in this condition. Now it is a reality, a certainty. I cannot control myself. Who will help me, who counsel me, to circumvent the inevitable?

EGMONT: Then hear me. If your soul is so powerfully bent on saving me, if you loathe the tyranny that has fettered me, save me! Every moment is precious. You are the son of him who has all power, you are yourself powerful— Let us flee! I know the roads; the means cannot be unknown to you. Only these walls, only a few miles separate me from my friends. Unlock these fetters, take me to them, and be ours. Certainly the King will one day thank you for saving me. Now he is taken by surprise, and perhaps knows nothing of all this. Your father dares it; and the King himself must approve it once it is done, even though it fill him with horror. You stand there thinking? Oh, think how I may be free! Speak, and feed hope in my yet living soul.

FERDINAND: Peace! Oh, be still! With every word you add to my despair. There is no way, no counsel, no escape. —It is that which tortures me, grips and rends my heart as with claws. I myself drew the net; I know its every harsh, firm knot, I know that the ways are barred to daring and to cunning alike. I am as much in fetters as you, as all the others. Should I lament, if I had not already tried everything? I threw myself at his feet, reasoned, implored. He sent me here, that all my pleasure in life and desire for life should perish in this instant.

EGMONT: There is no salvation?

FERDINAND: None.

EGMONT: (*stamping his foot*) No salvation!——Sweet life! Precious, familiar experience of being and acting! From you I must part! And part so passively. Not in the confusion of battle, amid the din of weapons, the excitement of combat do you fling me a hasty farewell; you take no hurried leave, shorten not the moment of parting. I must take your hand, look once more into your eyes, and, conscious of all your beauty, all your value, resolutely tear myself away and say: Go from me!

FERDINAND: And I must stand by and see it, and be unable to uphold you, unable to interfere! Oh, what voice could suffice to bewail it! What heartstrings would not melt at this grievous wrong!

EGMONT: Control yourself!

FERDINAND: You can control yourself, you can renounce, can grasp the hand of Fate and take the dire step with the courage of a hero. What can I do? What shall I do? You conquer yourself and us; you surpass; I survive you and myself. Amid the joy of the feast I have lost my light, my banner in the confusion of battle. The future rises before me drained of all savor, inextricable, overcast.

EGMONT: Young friend, whom, by a strange fate, I gain and lose at once, you who feel the anguish of death for me, who mourn for me, look upon me in these moments; you do not lose me. If my life was a mirror in which you liked to see yourself, let my death be even such to you. Men are not only together when they are side by side; he who is far away, he who has departed is alive for us too. I live for you, and have lived enough for myself. I have enjoyed every day; every day I have been prompt to do my duty as my conscience showed it to me. Now my life ends, as it might well have ended earlier, much earlier, even on the sands of Gravelines. I cease to live; but I have lived. Even so live you, my friend, eagerly and joyously, and dread not death.

FERDINAND: You could have preserved your life for us, you should have. You yourself have brought yourself to death. Often have I listened when wise men talked of you; friends or enemies to you, they argued long over your capacities; but in the end they all agreed, none dared deny it, all must needs admit, "Yes, he is treading a perilous path." How often I wished that I could warn you! Can it be that you had no friends?

EGMONT: I was warned.

FERDINAND: And how exactly the same were the accusations that I found in the indictment against you! And then your answers! good enough to excuse you, but not conclusive enough to exculpate you—

EGMONT: Enough of this. Men believe that they direct their lives, that they choose their own course; but the soul is irresistibly drawn in the direction of its fate. Let us not dwell on this; of such thoughts I can easily rid myself—not so easily of concern for my country; yet that too will be provided for. If my blood could be shed for many, could bring my people peace, it would be shed gladly. Unfortunately, that will not be the case. Yet it befits a man not to brood when he can no longer act. If you can control or guide your father's ruinous power, do it. But who can do that?—Farewell!

FERDINAND: I cannot leave you.

EGMONT: I ask you to do what you can for my followers. My servants are good men; may they not be forced to part, not fall into want! What can you tell me of Richard, my secretary?

FERDINAND: He has gone before you. He was beheaded as an accomplice in high treason.

EGMONT: Poor soul!—But one thing more, and then farewell; I am exhausted. However powerfully the mind may be preoccupied, nature in the end irresistibly demands her due; and as a child, even in the serpent's coils, enjoys refreshing sleep, so even at the gates of death the weary man lies down for the last time and sleeps his fill, as if a long journey yet lay before him.—But one thing more—I know a girl; you will not scorn her for having been mine. Now that I have entrusted her to you, I die easy. You have a noble nature; a woman who finds such a man is secure. Is my old Adolf still alive? Is he free?

FERDINAND: The hale old man who always attended you when you rode?

EGMONT: Yes.

FERDINAND: He lives and is free.

EGMONT: He knows her house; let him take you there, and then pension him to his dying day for having led you to such a treasure.—Farewell!

FERDINAND: I cannot go.

EGMONT: (*pushing him toward the door*) Farewell!

FERDINAND: Oh, let me stay a little—!

EGMONT: Friend, no leave-taking.

(*He goes to the door with* FERDINAND, *and there tears himself away.* FERDINAND, *stunned, hurries off.*)

EGMONT: (*alone*) Malignant man! Little did you think that you would confer this benefit on me through your son. Through him I am freed from cares and griefs, from fear and every anxious thought. Gently but urgently, Nature demands her final due. All is over, the die is cast! and what, being uncertain, last night held me waking on my cot now in its irresistible certainty lulls my every sense to sleep.

(*He sits down on the cot. Music*)

Sweet sleep! Like pure pleasure you come the more willingly the less you are besought and prayed for. You loose the knots of stern thoughts, mingle all shapes of joy and grief; the round of inner harmonies circles on unimpeded, and wrapped in pleasing delirium, we sink down, and cease to be.

(*He falls asleep; the music continues, accompanying his*

slumber. Behind his cot the wall seems to open, and a shining vision appears. FREEDOM, *in celestial raiment, surrounded by a halo of light, rests on a cloud. She has* CLARA'S *features, and bends toward the sleeping hero. Her bearing expresses a deep feeling of compassion, she seems to mourn over him. Presently she regains her composure and with an encouraging gesture shows him a sheaf of arrows and then a staff and hat. She bids him rejoice, and revealing to him that his death will secure freedom for the Provinces, she hails him as victor and holds out a laurel wreath. As her hand, holding the wreath, approaches his head,* EGMONT *makes a movement like one turning in his sleep, so that he lies with his face toward her. She holds the wreath suspended over his head; from far in the distance military music is heard, played on drums and fifes; at the first sound of it the vision vanishes. The music grows louder.* EGMONT *wakes; the prison is dimly lighted by the dawn. His first movement is to raise one hand to his head; still keeping it there, he stands up and looks about.)*

The wreath is gone! Fair vision, the light of day has frightened you hence! Yes, it was they, they together, the two sweetest joys of my heart in one. Divine freedom borrowed the shape of my beloved; the exquisite girl put on the heavenly raiment of my friend. At this solemn moment, they appear as one, more solemn than tender. She came before me with blood-stained feet, and the billowing folds of her robe were stained with blood. It was my blood and the blood of many noble hearts. No, it was not shed in vain. Forward, forward! Oh, my gallant people! The Goddess of Victory leads you! And as the sea breaks through your dykes, so you must break the wall of tyranny, tear it to pieces and with swelling flood sweep it from the soil that tyranny has usurped! (*The drums sound nearer.*)

Hark, hark! How often has that tone led my free steps to the field of combat and victory! How cheerfully did my comrades tread the path of danger and renown! I too go to meet an honorable death from this dungeon; I die for freedom, for which I lived and fought and to which I now offer myself in passive sacrifice.

(*The rear of the stage is occupied by a line of Spanish soldiers, carrying halberds.*)

Yes, bring them on, as many as you will! Close your ranks, you frighten me not. I am accustomed to standing with spears behind me and spears before me and, surrounded by menacing death, only to feel the courage that is life with doubled intensity.

(*Drums*)

The enemy hems you in on every side! Swords flash; friends, be your courage but the higher! Behind you are your parents, your wives, your children!

(*Pointing to the guards*) They are driven on only by their master's hollow word, not by their souls! Protect your possessions! And to save that which is dearest and most precious to you, fall joyously, as I shall set you the example. (*Drums. As he advances toward the guards and the door rear, the curtain falls; the orchestra strikes up and ends the play with a symphony of victory.*)

WORLD CLASSICS IN TRANSLATION

New modern translations of foreign language classics introduced by interpretations of authors, works, literary and historical backgrounds. Everyone who reads for pleasure and relaxation should augment his library of the world's best by these charming yet inexpensive books.

from the French

Andromache
by Racine pa. 95¢, cl. $2.95

Candide
by Voltaire pa. $1.25

Don Juan
by Molière pa. 95¢

Emile
by Rousseau pa. 95¢

Knock
by Romains pa. 95¢, cl. $2.95

My Friend's Book
by France pa. 95¢

Phaedra
by Racine pa. 75¢

Tartuffe
by Molière pa. 75¢, cl. $2.95

The Cid
by Corneille pa. 95¢, cl. $2.95

The Learned Ladies
by Molière pa. 95¢

The Marriage of Figaro and The Barber of Seville
by Beaumarchais pa. $1.25, cl. $2.95

The Middle-Class Gentleman
by Molière pa. 95¢

The Misanthrope
by Molière pa. 75¢, cl. $2.95

The Miser
by Molière pa. 75¢, cl. $2.95

The Pretentious Young Ladies
by Molière pa. 95¢

Topaze
by Pagnol pa. 75¢, cl. $2.95

from the Italian

Clizia
by Machiavelli pa. $1.25, cl. $2.95

from the Latin & Greek

Caesar's Gallic War
pa. $1.65, cl. $2.95

The Compact Homer
(The Iliad and The Odyssey)
Translation by S. H. Butcher, A. Lang, W. Leaf and E. Myers, with introduction by Mildred Marcett
pa. $1.95, cl. $4.25

from the Spanish

Classic Tales from Spanish America
pa. $1.50, cl. $2.95

Classic Tales from Modern Spain pa. $1.50, cl. $2.95

Doña Perfecta
by Galdos pa. 95¢

Jose
by Palacio Valdès pa. $1.25, cl. $2.95

La Gaviota (The Sea Gull)
by Caballero pa. 95¢, cl. $2.95

Life is a Dream
by Calderón pa. $1.25

Pepita Jiménez
by Valera pa. $1.25

Six Exemplary Novels
by Cervantes pa. $1.50, cl. $2.95

The Life of Lazarillo de Tormes
pa. 75¢

The Maiden's Consent
by Moratín pa. $1.25, cl. $2.95

The Mayor of Zalamea
by Calderón pa. 75¢

The Three-Cornered Hat
by Alarcón pa. $1.25

from the German

Egmont
by Goethe pa. 95¢, cl. $2.95

Emilia Galotti
by Lessing pa. 75¢, cl. $2.95

Germelshausen
by Gerstäcker pa. 95¢

Immensee
by Storm pa. 95¢, cl. $2.95

Love and Intrigue
by Schiller pa. $1.25, cl. $2.95

Mary Stuart
by Schiller pa. 95¢, cl. $2.95

Nathan de Weise
by Lessing pa. $1.25

Prince Frederick of Homburg
by von Kleist pa. $1.25, cl. $2.95

Urfaust
by Goethe pa. $1.25

William Tell
by Schiller pa. $1.25

BARRON'S EDUCATIONAL SERIES, INC. 113 Crossways Park Dr., Woodbury, N.Y.